BRAVE SONORA

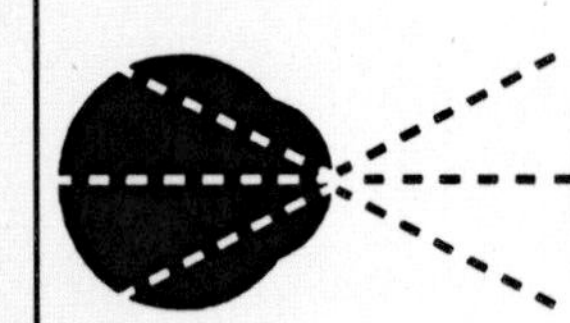

Brave Sonora

BLOOD FOR JUSTICE

Steven Law

WHEELER PUBLISHING
A part of Gale, Cengage Learning

Farmington Hills, Mich • San Francisco • New York • Waterville, Maine
Meriden, Conn • Mason, Ohio • Chicago

This is a work of fiction. Names, characters, places, and incidents either are the product of the author's imagination or are used fictitiously, and any resemblance to actual persons, living or dead, business establishments, events, or locales is entirely coincidental.

Wheeler Publishing Large Print Western.
The text of this Large Print edition is unabridged.
Other aspects of the book may vary from the original edition.
Set in 16 pt. Plantin.

LIBRARY OF CONGRESS CATALOGING-IN-PUBLICATION DATA

Law, Steven.
Brave sonora : blood for justice / Steven Law. — Large print edition.
pages cm — (Wheeler Publishing large print western)
ISBN 978-1-4104-6980-9 (softcover) — ISBN 1-4104-6980-8 (softcover)
1. Large type books. I. Title.
PS3612.A944338B73 2014
813'.6—dc23 2014018095

Published in 2014 by arrangement with The Berkley Publishing Group, a member of Penguin Group (USA) LLC, a Penguin Random House Company

Printed in the United States of America
1 2 3 4 5 18 17 16 15 14

For L. D. Clark, my young friend

In memory of Georgia Hazel Anderson
and Shane Michael Anderson

. . . on the point he maintained, that knights-errant were what the world stood most in need of, and that in him was to be accomplished the revival of knight errantry.

— Miguel de Cervantes, *Don Quixote*

Chapter One

JANUARY 26, 1884
Hermosillo, Sonora, Mexico

The shod hooves of the two bay horses made a rhythmic echo as Enrique Osorio and Sereno trotted down the cobblestone street in front of Plaza Zaragoza. The morning air was cool but the sun was already warming the earth, to the point where Enrique was glad that he only wore his bolero jacket over a cotton shirt. His sombrero was not yet needed and hung on his back from a leather chin cord around his neck. Sereno's red headband, faded from years in the sun, was distinct around his long, silky black hair that draped over the shoulders of his buckskin shirt. He was no longer the Tohono O'odham wilderness boy that had followed Enrique around for so many years, but had filled out into a man's clothes, with a square jaw and a handsome brow. He also wore a white cotton scarf, tied as the headband was, around his neck to cover the scar created by the throat slashing that took his voice as a child.

Enrique cast an admiring gaze at the *Catedral de la Asunción,* and at the newly constructed governmental palace, but foremost on his mind was the *Hacienda de Ramírez,* an orange and cotton plantation outside of Hermosillo, near the foothills of the Bacoachito mountain. His attention was drawn to the distant peaks, barely visible through the morning haze, and then he thought about the information he had received about where his grandfather, Isidro Jesus de la Rosa, was last seen working on this plantation.

When they reached the long lane leading to the *hacienda,* Enrique looked over at Sereno, who acknowledged that this was the time to take their necessary precautions. The two riders would no longer ride side-by-side, but Sereno would fall back two horse lengths, having Enrique's back.

The two men rode down the lane bordered by fan palms, a good one hundred yards from a white adobe structure. Spacious orange groves stood on each side of the palms and extended a good four hundred yards in both directions. Occasional workers in broad-brimmed straw hats stopped their labor to take a quick glance at the visitors. The adobe structures at the end of the lane made up the main dwelling of the plantation, with a frontal colonnade, a chapel with a mission-style bell on the far right side, and farther to the right a more modest, lengthy adobe with several doors that Enrique was sure were the servants' or workers' quarters. As they rode closer to the end of the lane they saw a woman sitting on a knee-high, circular stone basin, filling clay pots with water and placing them on a cart pulled by a burro.

Two guards in all-white cotton wearing large sombreros and bandoleers stood near the center of the colonnade, holding rifles across their forearms. Sereno stopped at the opening of the lane and Enrique continued riding toward the guards. They raised their rifles and held them ready in both hands as Enrique approached.

He brought his horse to a halt ten yards from the guards, close enough to see their attentive eyes. The one on the left kept glancing at Sereno.

Enrique nodded to the guard on the right. "Santiago Ramírez?"

The guard hesitated then nodded toward the chapel. Enrique looked in that direction where a spray of red, yellow, and white flowers stood on an easel outside the entrance, and another guard was posted there just like the ones in front of him. Enrique nodded his thanks to the guard and nudged his horse toward the chapel.

He stopped near a hitching rail and dismounted, removed his sombrero from behind his neck and hung it on the horn of the saddle. As he stepped toward the chapel entrance he looked up at the arched bell tower and immediately thought of Father Gaeta back at Tumacácori, and couldn't help noticing how much smaller the bell was here, than the one back home at the mission.

The guard raised his chin and stood more erect when Enrique approached and as before, he asked for Santiago Ramírez. The guard immediately nodded his head backward, and Enrique went on behind him and entered the chapel. Once his eyes adjusted to the darker room, he noticed a wooden casket at the end of the center aisle, between the pews and at the front of the sanctuary. There was another spray of flowers on the casket, and at least a dozen people filled the front pews.

Enrique stepped slowly down the aisle until he neared the front pews, and an older man, likely in his sixties, black hair slicked and parted, wearing a dark suit, stood up at the end of the pew to greet him. He looked at Enrique with serious black eyes.

"Con permiso," Enrique said. "I am looking for Santiago Ramírez."

"I am Jose Flores." Jose's chin drooped slightly as he looked back at a woman who sat near him, her salt and pepper hair partially covered by a black lace veil. He leaned down and whispered in her ear. When she turned her face bore tears of sadness, but she stood to acknowledge the visitor.

"I am Constanza Ramírez. Who are you?"

"I am sorry to intrude, *señora.* I am Enrique Osorio, and I am looking for my grandfather, Isidro Jesus de la Rosa, who I have heard works for Santiago Ramírez on this plantation."

"Si," Constanza said. "I knew your grandfather. He did work here a short while. He was our cook . . . and a very good one. But he was taken by Arriquibar Sosa for payment of a debt that my late husband refused to pay." Señora Ramírez turned her head slowly toward the casket.

Enrique felt a tingle in his stomach. It had been so long since he had seen his grandfather. Could he really have found him? But he could not forget his manners, so he quickly acknowledged that he was at a wake. "Your husband . . . he has recently passed?"

Constanza turned her head quickly back toward Enrique, with a look of both fear and anger. "He was murdered! Crucified by that evil *oficial,* Sosa."

Enrique took a deep breath and glanced at the casket, then back at Señora Ramírez. "You have my deepest sympathies, *señora.* Please allow me to pay my respects, then I would ask how I could find this Señor Sosa."

Before Señora Ramírez could answer, the guard from outside came running down the aisle toward them. "*Señora!* Sosa's men . . . they are riding down the lane!"

Along with the rest of the funeral attendants, Enrique followed Constanza and Jose down the aisle and out of the chapel. When they reached the doorway at least twenty riders, all wearing khaki, military style uniforms, except for one, the lead rider, who wore a white suit and a bone colored felt hat, rode into the courtyard raising a large cloud of dust. They all wore black, polished riding boots with uppers to the knees. Four of the men stopped near the entrance to the lane, dust clouding around them, and the rest spread out in a line that stretched from the palms by the orange grove to the main house.

Enrique squinted and peered through the dust cloud for Sereno, but he was nowhere to be found. He was certain that the Tohono O'odham was not far away, but simply keeping out of sight to avoid trouble.

Constanza stepped out into the courtyard and glared at the lead rider, who stepped down off his horse, as did one of the other riders who came to hold the reins for him. The man took off black leather gloves that were a clear contrast to his all white suit, but a perfect match to his boots. Silence fell upon the plantation save for the whickering of the horses and the rubbing of saddle leather.

Señora Ramírez glanced back at Enrique. "Well, Señor Osorio, you will not need to travel far to find Arriquibar Sosa." She turned her head back toward the man in white. "The man and all his vileness stands before us now."

Enrique stepped beside Constanza, as did Jose. They all looked directly at Sosa, who smirked as he walked toward them, but most notable were his green eyes and lighter skin, with an appearance more like a Spaniard than a Mexican.

Sosa removed his hat and bowed his head slightly as he looked at Señora Ramírez. "My deepest sympathy and respect, *señora.*"

Constanza spat on the ground at his feet. "How dare you show your face at this wake. Murderer!" Jose grabbed her arm as if trying to hold her back.

Sosa looked down at the ground where she spat, then raised his eyebrows as he returned his hat to his head. "It is not my fault that your husband would not abide by my rules. Rules should be made to live by, not to die by."

"We will never agree to your policies or your corrupt *oficiales.* Get off our *hacienda,* now!"

"I am sorry you see things that way, *señora.* But I still have unfinished business. Business that now involves your eldest son."

"He will never show his face to you. Because of you he is forced into hiding and can't even attend his own father's funeral."

"Yes, that is too bad. All he had to do was surrender to me and he would be attending the funeral right now, mourning at his mother's side. But, instead, he chooses to do things the difficult way."

Before Constanza could respond, a loud scream came from the yard in front of the servants' quarters. The funeral party all scurried toward the alleyway where the scream came from and Enrique followed them more slowly, glancing back at Sosa who stood still among the mounted *oficiales* staring contemptuously at Constanza Ramírez.

When they reached the alleyway Jose had to hold Constanza to keep her from collapsing onto the dusty ground. Enrique picked up his pace to find Constanza fainted in Jose's arms, and before them a sorrel horse standing with the reins dragging the ground in front of him. Next to the horse was a body of a man lying chest down on the ground, his head sideways, covered by dust and eyes half open, and a bone-handled knife was sticking out of his back.

Enrique ran to the body and felt the neck for a pulse. He looked gravely back at Jose, who had tears running down his cheeks as he held Señora Ramírez over his knees.

"It is her son," Jose said.

Enrique felt the tension rise to his neck, and he quickly thought of the breathing lessons that his friend and Chinese comrade Pang Lo had taught him. He took a deep breath in, then let it out slowly from his nose and looked down the alleyway at Sosa, who had now remounted his horse and nudged it toward them. The military party followed him at an equal pace.

Enrique made firm eye contact with Jose.

"Take care of the *señora,* and when she is well let her know that I am at her service."

"I think I have heard of you," Jose said. "Are you not the one of *El Trio*? *Los héroes* who brought down Antonio Valdar?"

Enrique had never heard of himself nor his comrades referred to as *"El Trio."* He never knew that the word of their daring efforts had reached all the way to Hermosillo. But he wondered who the *trio* meant? Since indeed there were four men, and not three. Were they referring to Sheriff Dutton or Sereno? Surely *El Trio* included Pang Lo. Regardless, there was only one way Enrique could answer the question.

"*Si,* Señor Flores. Me and my friends . . . we tracked down Valdar and his evil *compadres* and sent them all to their graves."

"Your legend is well-known here. It is a blessing that you have come to us."

Enrique was a bit overwhelmed by the expectations of this man, and he was a little apprehensive toward offering too much in the way of assistance. Tracking and killing Valdar and his men had been an amazing feat, but a corrupt *oficial* and his army of men were a much different, if not steeper, mountain to climb. Yet the sadness and pure desperation in Jose's eyes stirred all of Enrique's fears and concerns. Besides, Sosa was holding his grandfather prisoner. He had to do something, and regardless of the grand challenge that now stood before him, he felt like he belonged here. He could not, however, do so much alone. He had to find Pang Lo, who was many hours away in Tucson, but he could send Sereno to get him. He was not sure, though, if Chas Dutton could be found. After he resigned as Pima County Sheriff, he had gone back to Missouri to visit his brother and work on the farm and stayed there. If not, then the legend would be correct now. They were not four, but *"El Trio."*

Sosa and his militia rode up to the scene and the riders surrounded them. Jose remained on one knee, embracing Señora Ramírez who lay unconscious over his thigh. Enrique took three steps away from the dead body and stood in front of Jose.

Sosa looked down at the body and shook his head. "Such a sad situation. It seems that things are falling apart around here."

"No," Enrique said. "They will all be just fine."

Sosa tilted his head slightly and raised his eyebrows as he looked at Enrique. "You seem very sure of yourself. And who might you be?"

"I am Enrique Osorio. I am here looking

for my grandfather, Isidro Jesus de la Rosa. I have knowledge that he is working for you."

Sosa leaned forward. "Working?" He raised his head, nearly looking at the sky, and laughed loudly. Several of the military party broke out in laughter with him. But it was all short-lived as Sosa's smiling face dwindled and he took a deep breath and studied Enrique.

"This name, Osorio. I have heard of you, no?"

The soldier mounted to Sosa's right leaned closer to him and whispered. Sosa's eyes widened slightly as he looked back at Enrique inquiringly. "Antonio Valdar?" He said in a fake astonishment. "So you are one of those brave amigos. Well . . . gentlemen we are in the presence of a legend."

Enrique studied the faces of several of the men, and most of which were expressionless, except for the few that wore the seriousness of a prowling cat.

"It's interesting that you mention your grandfather," Sosa said. "We also have dealings with him."

"Whatever debt he has to you, I will pay it," Enrique said.

"Yes, yes. I suppose you will." Sosa was quick to nod at several of the riders behind

Enrique.

Enrique turned and got a quick look at each of them as they dismounted and surrounded him. He took a deep breath, and ascertained which one would strike first. One had a twitching eye and pinched lips, which no doubt meant he was the most impulsive. He wasn't sure about the others, but like Pang had taught him, after the first punch, with a clear focus, the instincts would take over. So he tested this man's restlessness. Sure enough as he lunged toward him and all Enrique had to do was lean sideways, extending his leg at an angle: the man tripped to a sprawling display on the ground. The man behind him and to his left was the next to move. Enrique was quick to crouch, then turn and jab an elongated hand into his face. The other two came quickly. Avoiding them was easier than fighting them, so at just the right moment, Enrique shifted his body and somersaulted away, only to rise back to his feet in a crouching stance, hands forward, as he watched both men crash into one another then fall to the ground. He scanned the area with wide-eyed attentiveness as all four hatless, glaring men, faces covered with dust, rose slowly to their feet. Before they could attack again, all of the other riders raised their rifles and pointed them directly at Enrique.

Sosa clapped slowly and condescendingly. "Very impressive. I could use a man with such talents. Come, be my guest for dinner tonight. And we will talk about your grandfather, and your future."

Enrique glanced at several of the soldiers as they glared down the barrels of their rifles. "I work for no man but myself. And my future is my own to plan."

Sosa nodded. "Yes, well that is unfortunate." He nodded to one of the men standing near him. "Arrest him. Let's see how our jail cell fits into his plans."

The four men quickly subdued Enrique, who did little to fight them, instead looking around for signs of Sereno. By the time they had his hands tied and mounted on his own horse, Enrique looked down at Jose, who looked back at him with sadness and great fear. Enrique nodded to him, which was all he could do to show his commitment to helping the Ramírez family, and to assure them he would return to demand the justice they desired and deserved.

ONE HOUR LATER
Tucson, Arizona Territory
Enrique was fortunate that Father Gaeta

had taught Sereno how to read and write, and together the three of them learned sign language. Though Sereno was the only one to eventually use it, it was certainly important for them to understand it. The loss of one's voice might inhibit communication in one form, but limitations often breed strengths in others.

Pang Lo was in his tent meditating when Vin Long came running in with the telegram messenger. The young Chinaman sat on a maroon silk pillow with his hands in a praying position, eyes closed, and a narrow plume of sandalwood incense rose from a table in front of him. Vin cleared his throat and Pang slowly opened one eye, then another, and then squinted with annoyance.

"There is an important message for you," Vin Long said.

The telegram messenger, a skinny young man with red hair and a hint of whisker growth, wearing a Western Union uniform, took one step closer to Pang and handed him the telegram. Pang did not take it, but instead, addressed the messenger.

"Read it to me," Pang said.

The messenger looked nervously back at Vin, who nodded, then he unfolded the telegram and began to read it aloud.

"Enrique is being held against his will in

Hermosillo. Stop. Keeping watchful eye but need your help. Stop. Please do not trouble Father Gaeta. Stop. Sereno. Stop."

Pang nodded then took a deep breath in through his nose, and glanced at the train ticket to San Francisco lying on a short legged table beside him. In one scissor-like move, Pang pushed himself up and put a hand on the messenger's shoulder. "Do you have the address of Chas Dutton?"

The messenger nodded. "Yes sir, I believe we do. He is in Missouri."

"Yes," Pang said. "I want you to take that telegram back and send the exact same message to Dutton, only with my name instead of Sereno's."

The messenger nodded again and turned swiftly to leave the tent.

"Wait," Pang said.

The messenger stopped abruptly and turned back to Pang. "You can leave out the part about troubling Father Gaeta."

"All right. Anything else?"

Pang looked at Vin and pondered a moment. "Yes. Right before my name, you can add, 'The weather is nice in Mexico this time of year. Stop.' " Pang winked at the messenger, who grinned before he turned and left the tent.

Vin stepped closer to Pang. "What about

sailing to Asia? You wanted to explore the Orient and all of its beauty."

Pang reached over and picked up the ticket, looked at it for a short moment then handed it to Vin. "Do you think Asia will still be beautiful when I get back?"

Vin laughed. "Ah, Pang Lo, you make good joke. I will take good care of ticket for you."

THE NEXT MORNING
Putnam County, Missouri

Chas Dutton stood on the other end of a crosscut saw from his older brother, Reginald — each man stripped from their woolen coats and cotton shirts, only the stained tops of their faded union suits covered their torsos, and their leather braces hung loose at their sides. Sweat poured from their brows despite the ten below zero wind chill and foot-deep snow all around them. Next to the debris of sawdust in the snow, a waist high pile of sixteen inch logs was building as they kept cutting, but even after the cutting was done, the splitting must commence. In this type of weather, wood cutting was never done.

Chas felt his brother's stride lag, and thought it odd since his brother was bigger and stronger, and had always outperformed him in physical duress, but when he looked at his brother's face that was when he realized it wasn't his wind giving out, but something had attracted his attention. Chas then slowed and they both stopped, and Chas turned to see what distracted their work. A horse and rider were high-stepping through the snow across the meadow and headed toward them. Chas wiped at his brow with his sawdust-smeared shirtsleeve then glanced back at his brother.

"You done?" Reginald said, one hand still firmly gripping the saw handle.

Chas paid him no mind, flipped his braces back over his shoulders, blew into his hands, and then looked back toward the rider and awaited his arrival.

Reginald rolled a cut log under his arm, then walked closer to the door of their cabin where an axe and an iron wedge leaned against the wall. He stood the oak log on its end in the snow then grabbed the axe, and in one fell swoop split it right down the middle. He split each half and split them again, and then picked up the sections and stacked them neatly on a nearby woodpile.

When the rider was close enough Chas recognized him as the youthful Harvey Patterson, a railroad depot attendant from nearby Unionville; a good five mile ride if he followed the roads. Patterson rode up to Chas and they each nodded for a greeting. The young man, bundled with a scarf tied over the top of his hat and underneath his chin, and another wrapped around his mouth, spoke through the woolen garment emitting a plume of steam.

"Telegram for you, Mr. Dutton." The lad leaned over without dismounting and handed the paper document to Chas.

Chas unfolded the paper and read it immediately, and then took a quick glance behind him at Reginald. The older brother made bold eye contact with Chas then set up another log and quickly swung the axe.

Chas looked back up at Patterson. "Best come in and warm up. Got some coffee on the stove. Maybe some stew left over . . . and biscuits."

"That's mighty kind of you, Mr. Dutton." The young man wasted no time dismounting.

Chas had stopped working long enough for his sweaty body to start chilling. He helped his brother pick up the split pieces of the log. "Let's warm up a bit."

"I'm plenty warm," Reginald said. "Besides, I 'spect you'll be heading back to Arizona, so I better keep at it."

Chas cocked half a grin and shook his

head. His brother wasn't only the bigger man, he was also the most perceptive. "I'll help you get a good supply done before I go. But I'll need to try and catch the afternoon train."

Reginald held the axe at his side and stared at his brother a moment. "That's mighty kind of you, Mr. Dutton."

"I'm sorry, Reggie. But a good friend is in trouble. They wouldn't have asked me to come if it wasn't serious."

Reginald tossed the axe until it landed hard against the wood pile. "Just like after the war . . . you can't decide which is more important, the frontier or your family."

The two men stared at each other a moment and then Reginald pulled up his braces and went inside the cabin. Patterson, who had been standing and waiting, stomping his feet and blowing into his hands, quickly followed him inside once Chas gave him the nod.

Chas unfolded the telegram and read it again. His feelings did not change. Reginald could survive without him. Enrique might not.

Chapter Two

Pang had learned that when traveling outside of the Chinese settlement it was best not to attract attention to his race. Dressed as an Anglo didn't work, because the hat brim was not wide enough to shade his appearance. The Mexican sombrero, however, was perfect for his cover. It was only when he was up close and had removed his hat or raised his head enough for them to see his face that his identity became evident. But then riding through the wilderness, down the trails and through the mountain passes, the deer, the cougar, the rattlesnakes, the peccary, the desert rats — they did not discriminate against him. Even when in the villages and cities, he was shaded enough that people only threw him a passing glance. The black hair under a straw sombrero, the serape, cotton trousers and leather boots, worn by a man on a horse, these were not so unfamiliar as to cause alarm.

It was no different when he arrived in Hermosillo. He rode peacefully into the town and onto the cobblestone streets. He did not know where to go, but he trusted Sereno enough to be on the lookout for his arrival. No one else but Sereno would recognize him, and would know what to look for. The horse, but more specifically the saddle, would be the first signs to give him away. But then, Pang was sure that Sereno would notice his queue — the braid of hair that hung from the back and draped over his shoulder to the front — that would only be noticeable to a careful eye.

When a stone hit the street in front of him and bounced off to his left, Pang stopped his horse and peered off to the right. Sure enough, there was Sereno, leaning against the side of an adobe building, and once their eyes met, Sereno went behind the building and into an alley. Pang reined his horse in that direction, and when he reached the alley he followed Sereno's path as he zigzagged swiftly between buildings, and to another street that led to a livery. There Sereno stood, in front of the livery, waiting for him.

Pang dismounted and Sereno took the reins of his horse and led it inside the livery. Pang followed him in and they paid the

Mexican attendant, who had to take a second glance at Pang when he realized he looked different. Pang paid the man an extra peso and then followed Sereno to a stall where he immediately noticed Enrique's horse, and he rubbed a hand down his neck. He turned back to Sereno, who used sign language that indicated capture, and many men. Sereno led Pang back to the main double doors and pointed toward a large adobe structure across the street, where the doorways were protected by armed guards. Pang nodded as he understood that Enrique was in that building.

Even though he had asked for Chas Dutton to come, Pang did not wait around for his reply knowing he couldn't wait the three or four more days it would take for his arrival. What Pang did not know was why Enrique was being held, or who and what he would be up against when he tried to free him. It was a touchy situation, but there was not enough information yet to ascertain how difficult it was to be.

Before crossing the street Pang went back inside the livery and did his stretching and breathing exercises. The attendant was fetching grain and water and looking on at the Chinaman's unfamiliar activity. Sereno waited by the door, his eyes on the building and the guards. Though Pang tried not to let the attendant notice, he kept a peripheral view on him and his every move. Since Pang had come to town, this man was the only one who had seen him close enough to know he was a stranger. There was a lot of risk in him having this knowledge, therefore it would have to be dealt with responsibly.

When Pang was finished with his exercises, he met Sereno in the doorway.

"You stay here," Pang said. "Keep an eye on this man, and if he leaves, get our horses. You will know what to do."

Pang gave Sereno a gentle pat on the shoulder and then walked out into the street. When he got within twenty feet of the guards, the uniformed men stood erect, held their guns firmly and blocked his passage. After they got a closer look at Pang, they narrowed their eyes and exchanged glances with one another. Pang politely nodded.

"I am here to speak with Señor Sosa," Pang said. "He is holding my friend, Enrique Osorio."

The men looked at each other again, and then one of them nodded backward allowing him to go through the doorway, but they followed him. Once inside one of the guards stepped in front and led Pang across the stone tiled floor to another guard, who sat at a desk in front of a doorway. Due to his brass pendants and insignias above the pockets of his tunic, Pang assumed that this guard was of a higher ranking.

Both guards thrust their feet together and saluted the officer, and he returned the salute more casually, without standing from his chair, but with his eyes fixed on Pang.

"Quién eres?" asked the seated officer.

"I am Pang Lo." Pang bowed slightly. "I am here to inquire about my friend, Enrique Osorio, who I understand has been arrested."

The guard twitched a slight grin. "Ah yes, you are one of *El Trio.*"

Pang squinted his eyes. "I beg your pardon?"

The guard now stood and placed his hands on his hips, looking the Chinaman up and down. "The men who captured and killed Antonio Valdar. You do not know your own legend?"

Pang shook his head. "No, I have not heard of this name. It does not make sense, because trio means three, and we are four."

The guard now crossed his arms and nodded. "Ah, yes, this is correct. There was a gringo with you, not this . . ." He pointed toward the door with his chin. ". . . this

Apache at the livery across the street."

Pang tried not to act surprised. "No, he is one of us also. But he is Tohono O'odham, not Apache."

"Whatever you say," the guard said, stepping out from behind his table. "I am sure Señor Sosa will be interested to make your acquaintance." He pointed toward the door with his hand. "Please, come with me." He looked back sternly at the guards who acted as though they would also follow. "Back to your posts! *Ahora, rápidamente!*"

Though Pang was pleased that he now had two less men to worry about, after he walked through the door and saw the many armed guards that stood in front of entrances to many rooms, two more would have been no more trouble. He counted eight, all with rifles, and black holsters at their sides holding pistols. Though Pang had a lot of confidence in his Kung Fu, he was not one to take firearms for granted. It was a fantasy to believe that the human response time was any match for a bullet from a gun. There was only the chance of a bad aim, but the more guns there were, the more chances that someone's aim would meet its target. No, Pang did not take these things lightly. But what he did believe was that the strength was not in the bullets, or the guns they came from, but in the mind that controlled them. It was there, Pang knew, that he had to concentrate. To get those minds on a different course was a powerful strategy, and from what stood before him now, there were a lot of minds to distract.

What Pang also knew was that the stronger mind was the one of the leader. These men that stood before him now were mere puppets, and were no match for the one who held the strings. It was Sosa he would have to evaluate, and the men that stood closely to his side.

The officer walked up to a round topped wooden door within the white adobe wall of the hallway. There was a guard on each side of the door, and one directly across. The officer knocked and the door was opened slightly for a moment, then completely.

"Patrón," the officer said. "It is one of *El Trio."*

Pang stepped into the opening and Sosa, dressed in all white — trousers, shirt, and vest — stood from his desk smiling and holding a thick, smoldering cigar in his hand.

Pang removed the sombrero from his head and let it hang from the chin cord to his back.

"Ah yes," Sosa said. "I heard there was a

Chinaman among you. A Chinaman who now dresses as a Mexican." Sosa walked from behind the desk to the front and stood within a few feet from Pang. The armed guard that opened the door now stood behind Pang. Yes, Pang thought, it was a good strategy . . . to put a man in his blind spot.

"I would like you to meet Rufino," Sosa said, pointing his cigar toward the guard. Pang had to look up to make eye contact. He was indeed a tall man, and broad at the shoulders, with a thick brow and boney jaws that formed a permanent frown. To most men, Rufino would definitely be intimidating.

"I assume this is your first time in Hermosillo?" Sosa said.

"Yes," Pang said. "I have had no reason to come here until now."

"Yes, of course. So what do you know about this city? Or, more importantly, what do you know about me?"

Pang shrugged. "Nothing, really. Except that you are holding my friend prisoner for no good reason."

Sosa grunted. "Is this so?"

"It is what I am told, yes."

"Well, whoever is giving you this information is very confused. You see, this is my city. Nothing happens here without my knowing, or . . . without my permission. This friend of yours tried to stick his nose into my business, which . . ." Sosa smiled and held the cigar close to his mouth. ". . . which is not a wise thing to do."

"I am sorry, Señor Sosa, but I will have to disagree with you."

"Disagree? With *me*?"

"Yes. You see, my friend, Enrique, he came here on business of his own. I know him well enough to know that he would not care about anyone else's business, unless, of course, there was . . . as they say, a conflict of interest."

Sosa smiled, then laughed wildly. "Ah, yes. A conflict of interest! Well, this is exactly what has happened. But, I am a man who only likes to do business if I think there is something good in it for me. I told this friend of yours that I could use the skills of a man like him. Well, for that matter, *men,* like *El Trio.* Anyone who has the courage, and the skills, to take down Antonio Valdar . . . and his men?" Sosa raised his hands in the air and looked toward the ceiling. "*Dios mio!* They are men who could be a blessing to my work."

"This, I understand," Pang said. "So I presume that my friend turned down this offer from you, and that is why he is prisoner here?"

"Very perceptive of you. Perhaps you can change his mind?"

Pang shook his head. "This is not possible. I trust my friend's judgment completely. If he says no, then I am sure it is the right answer."

Sosa grunted slightly and grinned. "By the way, I am wondering. Why would you do such a thing?" Sosa said, waving the cigar up and down in front of Pang, and then putting it in his mouth and taking a deep drag. He followed with an exhale of a thick cloud of smoke and a squint of his eyes.

"Do what?" Pang said.

Sosa smiled for a moment. "Try to deceive us. A Chinaman dressed as a Mexican. I admit, it worked very well for a moment. But then, I smelled you. It is a foul stench, no?" Sosa looked at Rufino and laughed loudly. The guard followed with deep, gurgling grunt. Pang thought only to further his deception and blend into the laughter. He tipped his head back and laughed louder than both men, which caused Sosa to draw an immediate frown, set the cigar in a stone tray on his desk, and then walk back around to his seat but not sit down.

"Let's get something straight," Sosa said. "I will not be mocked. Not by anyone. Such things get you killed."

"I am sorry, Señor Sosa," Pang said, his face now calm and his eyes focused. "But where I come from no man has the right to insult another man in such a manner, or he is not a man, but a snake. So I have already learned a lot about you."

Sosa shared a sneering glance with Rufino, then gazed contemptuously at the Chinaman. "You say such things, which makes me wonder about your intelligence. I can only assume you came here for your friend . . . this — Osorio. But you walk in here and say such things, which will not help your friend; it will only get you killed."

"No, Señor Sosa. You will kill me anyway."

Sosa tilted his head and raised his eyebrows. "Maybe you are not so stupid?"

"No, because whatever it is you want, you will not get from us. So why waste time talking about such things? I think it is time to, as they say, 'get down to business.' "

Sosa narrowed his eyes and clenched his mouth, and made a quick glance to Rufino. Pang closed his own eyes, shutting out his sense of sight, and as his father had taught him to do, all of his concentration was focused on one sense — that from his ears.

For all Pang knew, there was no other sound in the room, other than the heartbeat and the deep inhale of breath from Rufino behind him. The movement of his arms, from the sound of the fabric of his tunic rubbing against his torso, was clear only to Pang. The sound was stronger on his right side, which quickly transferred to a clicking of metal and wood . . . that of his rifle. It cut through the air so swiftly that Pang knew now to open his eyes, and look above him at the haze of cigar smoke, which from the officer's motion parted four feet above his right shoulder, and confirmed what his ears had told him.

Faster than anyone could see, Pang raised his right elbow, blocking the stock of the rifle that the guard tried to use to strike Pang on the back of the head. A quick pivot allowed Pang to grab the rifle with both hands and spin it swiftly, the stock of the rifle striking the guard on the side of the chin. Rufino fell back against the door, closing it loudly, and he looked wide-eyed and angry back at the Chinaman. Before he could do anything about it, Pang grabbed both of Rufino's large hands, pulled them together, and with a loud growl and sprawling stance, Pang spun around and lifted the big man completely over his head and slammed him into Sosa's desk. Sosa fell backward into his chair in astonishment.

This drew the attention of the guards outside, who one by one tried to enter the room, but each time the door opened Pang kicked up a foot and slammed the door into their faces, knocking them down. Whenever one fell unconscious he counted, and when he got to eight, he knew that there was still one more, Rodríguez, who was smart enough not to try the same thing as the guards, who kept failing in their attempt. Pang was certain the officer was behind the door, waiting, with his pistol drawn, and sure enough, he pounded on the door calling out *"Patrón! Patrón!"*

In a sudden back flip, Pang landed on the desk, crouching on his feet, above the unconscious guard. Beside him was the cigar, which had fallen from the stone tray onto the wooden top, but it still smoldered. He grabbed the cigar quickly, then jumped from the desk onto the floor in front of Sosa.

Sosa threw his hands in the air, at shoulder height, as the Chinaman stood above him, holding the cigar as if it were a dart.

Sosa cocked a half grin. "*Very* impressive."

"Call him away from the door," Pang said. "Or I introduce each one of your eyes to eternal blindness."

Sosa studied Pang's intent stare. "You realize that you may win this battle, but after you leave here, it is only a matter of time before you and all of . . . *El Trio* . . . are dead men."

"I will take my chances. Call him off. Now!"

His hands still slightly raised, Sosa nodded slowly. "Colonel Rodríguez! Lower your weapon. Let this man go in peace."

"Tell him to empty his weapons. Open the door so I can see. I want to see and hear the bullets hitting the stone floor."

Sosa tilted his head, and Pang grabbed him by the hair and held the cigar an inch from his eye.

"Colonel!" Sosa yelled. "Open the door."

Rodríguez did as Sosa ordered. Pang stared at him while he hovered over Sosa.

"Empty the ammo from your weapons," Sosa said. "All of them."

Pang looked on as Rodríguez ejected the cartridges from his rifle and set it on the floor, and then he popped out the cylinder of his revolver and dumped the bullets. He set the pistol slowly on the floor.

"Now there is one more . . . condition," Pang said.

"Oh? You are making conditions now?"

"I am not leaving here without Enrique."

"And how do you propose to do such a thing?"

"This man . . . Colonel Rodríguez . . . he will get him and bring him here. Meanwhile, we will stay here and ponder the future of your eyesight until he returns."

It took less than two minutes for Colonel Rodríguez to return with Enrique, who rubbed his wrists from the soreness of handcuffs. He looked at the guards outside the door rubbing their foreheads and then looked through the doorway and smiled at his friend.

"What took you so long?" Enrique said. "I count only nine men, not counting Señor Sosa. You are getting sloppy, amigo."

"Yes, well," Pang said. "I think I stubbed my toe on the door."

The other guards lay on the floor moaning, starting to come to consciousness, including Rufino.

Enrique noticed the ammo cartridges lying on the floor. "Ah, yes, this is a good idea." He reached down and grabbed one of the guard's pistols out of the holster, rolled the cylinder and checked to see if it was loaded, and then waved it at Rodríguez. "Get all of the guns from your guards and empty them. Don't try anything foolish."

Pang lifted Sosa from the chair and

pushed him out into the hallway, then Rufino.

Enrique nodded at Sosa. "I am sorry it came to this. And now I must insist on the whereabouts of my grandfather."

Sosa laughed. "You are all full of demands!" He tried to walk closer to Enrique, but Pang quickly grabbed him by the throat and put the cigar under his right eye.

Enrique pointed at the cigar. "Amigo, you might want to puff on that a bit before it goes out."

Pang's eyes rounded and he looked at the ashy tip of the cigar.

Rodríguez saw this as an opportunity and lunged toward Enrique for the pistol, but not before Enrique completed a roundhouse punch to the jaw, and when the officer hit the floor Enrique dropped to one knee and pushed the barrel of the pistol under his chin. "Ah, *señor,* I can see you cannot be trusted."

When Enrique turned back to Pang, the Chinaman puffed hurriedly on the cigar, emitting large clouds of smoke. Sosa had lowered his hands and was about to attempt a move on Pang.

"Ah, *patrón,*" Enrique said, cocking the pistol. "That would not be wise."

Pang pulled the smoldering cigar away

from his mouth and looked at it admiringly. "Hmm. Not bad." He put the cigar back into his mouth, bit into it and looked back at Sosa. *"Gracias."*

Enrique grabbed Rodríguez by the back of the shirt collar and lifted him to his feet. After the officer removed all of the ammunition from the rifles and pistols, Enrique ordered them all to stand and walk.

"What are we doing with them?" Pang said.

"They may not have guns, but they still have legs, and I am sure a storage of more guns and ammunition somewhere. So, I am thinking that it is time Sosa has a tour of his own jail cell."

Sosa grinned as Enrique stared at him. "There are other men here . . . many all over the city, who on my single command will kill you instantly."

"I am sure this is true," Enrique said. He looked at Pang. "This man is proud of himself, no?"

Pang nodded. "Yes, he is proud of many things."

Enrique waved the pistol toward Sosa. "Pang, lead him toward the jail cells. We will follow you. And Sosa, when we encounter more of your men, make them drop their weapons. *Entiendes amigo?*"

Pang led them all down the hallway, and when they entered the cell area Sosa did as Enrique had said, and two guards dropped all of their weapons.

Enrique waved his gun toward the empty cell that he had once occupied. "All of you, in there."

There was barely enough room in the cell for all of them, but they crammed themselves inside. Pang took the ring of keys off of the guard, then closed the iron door and locked it.

Enrique picked up the guns that the guards had dropped and cartridges bounced on the tile floor as he emptied them of all ammunition. He also emptied the one he was carrying and dropped it on the floor. He walked up to the cell door and peered in at Sosa. "This is your last chance. Tell me where my grandfather is."

Sosa laughed. "Last chance? For what?"

"It is very simple, *señor.* I came here for my grandfather. That is all. I did not come here for this. It is of your choosing. Lead me to my grandfather and then I will take him and leave, and I am sure your guards will get you out of this cell in due time. Then, it will be as if nothing ever happened, and life is back to normal for all of us. But, if you choose to make it more difficult, then

I will promise you a fight like no other you have ever experienced."

Sosa laughed, as did Rufino, Rodríguez, and many of the guards with them.

Enrique looked at Pang. "Very well. Amigo, I do think I noticed some cans of kerosene in another room." Enrique looked sternly back at Sosa. "Retrieve them, and douse these men . . . then I am sure we can find something to light a fire."

All of the men in the cell lost their smug grins and their eyes widened. All except for Sosa, who stared contemptuously.

Pang puffed heavily on the cigar then removed it from his mouth and looked admiringly at the smoldering tip. "You know, I believe you are right."

"All right!" Sosa said. "Your grandfather is working in a tavern and restaurant that I own, on the north edge of the city. It is called *Casa del Norte.*"

Enrique studied Sosa's sincerity, and then stepped closer and peered at him through the steel bars. "*Muy bien.* Now I hope, Señor Sosa, for your sake, this is the truth. And that me and my amigos will find him there, and will not be pulled into a trap. Because if this happens . . . oh, *señor,* it would not be good for you."

Sosa sneered back at Enrique. "I guess

this is what you call a moment of uncertainty, no?"

Enrique nodded and backed away. *"Vamos."*

Enrique and Pang ran back into the hallway, and to the main entrance, where they met the guards standing outside. Pang bowed slightly, and then put his sombrero back on his head. *"Gracias, amigos."*

Sereno rode up quickly, both Pang and Enrique's horses tethered to his.

"I guess this means he had trouble in the livery." Pang said.

Suddenly, a voice sounded off from across the street. They all looked in that direction, and there, among several more of Sosa's *policía,* was the livery attendant, pointing at them.

"Well, amigo," Enrique said. "Do we run, or do we fight."

"I don't like guns," Pang said.

"I guess that means we fight."

Three uniformed men charged across the street toward them, and one of them yelled loudly to the other guards. *"Detener a esos hombres!"*

Pang and Enrique stepped back and faced the guards, who tried to raise their rifles, but in a flash Pang and Enrique took them right out of their hands, and like a perfectly choreographed duo, swung the stock ends upward and knocked each guard upside their heads. They fell cold.

Pang and Enrique turned quickly, only to watch Sereno lead the tethered horses in front of the charging officers, wrapping them in confusion and causing them to fall to the ground in a cloud of dust. Pang and Enrique ran for their horses, but not before seizing the officer's weapons and ejecting the ammunition onto the ground.

Enrique leaned over to one of them, who was spitting dust from his mouth. "*Lo siento,* but you should not play with guns in this way. Someone could get hurt."

Pang and Enrique mounted their horses and the three men spurred them to a gallop and headed east down the street. The three guards rose in a scramble trying to find the bullets that were scattered along the ground and load them back into their rifles, but it was no use. *El Trio* was gone.

Chapter Three

The three men rode at a gallop north out of town, and Sereno led them out of the flat valley and toward the foothills of the mountains. It was there, among the mesquite and thornscrub, where they would have good cover. They slowed to a lope as they reached the thick stands of head-high trees and Sereno turned to see if they were being followed. They all stopped and looked, but there was no one to be seen.

Sereno found a deer trail and they wove their way through the scrub for over an hour before they felt far enough off the main trail to make camp. When they stopped, Sereno dutifully took their horses and tied them to a mesquite tree, then unsaddled them.

Pang spread his feet apart and stretched toward the sky, then reached down and touched his toes.

Enrique put his hands on his hips and grinned at Pang. "Would you really have put that cigar in his eyes?"

Pang stopped stretching, looked up into the sky and shrugged. "If my life was in danger, I could probably do anything."

"I must admit, I was a bit surprised to hear that coming from you."

"It was a difficult situation, and I could tell a man like him must be dealt with very seriously."

"Yes, this man, Sosa, he is a bad man. But not like Valdar — people are not as scared, and he is very public."

Pang slowly rolled his head in circles, stretching the muscles in his neck. "But he still rules by fear. This I can tell."

"Yes, you are right. But he also provides a better life to those who are loyal to him. There is no way to make such a living in Mexico, and the people are willing to trade for it. To be a soldier in his army . . . well, his *policía* . . . is the best job in town."

Pang sat on the ground and stretched his legs straight out in front of him, then leaned forward and touched his toes. "To me, that is how we break his strength."

"What are you saying?"

"His *loyal* followers," Pang said. "We convince them not to follow him any more."

"The only way to do that is to offer them something better."

Pang stopped stretching, put his hands on the ground at his side and looked up at Enrique. "Is it not better to live without fear?"

Enrique nodded then reached out a hand to help Pang up. "Come on, amigo. Let's gather some wood."

Pang nodded, jumped to his feet, and walked along with Enrique. "I do not understand this *'El Trio'* name they have given us."

"I heard this, too," Enrique said. "People, they talk, and their words spread like a swarm of bees."

"But it is such a plain name. Not like 'The Three Musketeers,' or *'Tres Caballeros,'* you know?"

"I do not care about any name. Such things do not matter to me."

"Well, but at least they can get it right, you know? We were four, not three."

"They did not consider Sereno. He was very young, and did not ride among us, but close by. And now Señor Dutton is gone. So we are truly three."

"Not if Dutton comes here to help us."

"Why would he do that?"

"I sent him a telegram and told him that you were in trouble."

Enrique stopped and looked straight at

Pang. "You should not have done that."

"Why? He is our friend, too."

"But he went to his homeland, to return to his family. You should not leave him with such guilt."

"If he is loyal to his family then he will not come here, he will stay."

"It is not so much about loyalty, *mi* amigo, as it is about friendship. He is a good friend to us, and we should be good friends also by not interfering with his life."

"I did not know how bad things would be with you. What if I got captured, too? Then someone else would know, and we would have another chance for someone to help us."

Enrique nodded. "Yes, I see your point. But we do not need him now. It would be a very long journey for no reason."

"This is not over. We don't know that Sosa gave us good information. It could be another trap."

"Yes, I understand," Enrique said. "Which is why we need to get to this *Casa del Norte* quickly."

"Do you have a plan?"

"I have been thinking about it, yes. But there is something else that bothers me greatly. Tomorrow, I need to pay a visit to Constanza Ramírez. I have great concern for her and her rancho."

"Who is Constanza Ramírez?"

"She is a widow, on a plantation where my grandfather worked. That is why I went there. But Sosa killed her husband, and now her oldest son. Sosa took my grandfather, because this is what he does. And now, he is trying to take the plantation from Señora Ramírez."

"Is it good to get involved with such a thing? When you are so close to finding your grandfather?"

Enrique looked Pang directly in the eyes for a short moment. "If you would have seen what I have seen, you would feel like I do. Someone needs to stop this Sosa before he destroys all of Hermosillo."

"And we are the men to stop him?"

Enrique shrugged. "Now that you are here, it is possible. We have already proven we can outwit him."

"But it appears he has men all over town, and many guns."

"Yes, the *policía* are all under his control. As are many other people in Hermosillo."

"So, how will *El Trio* take on such an army of men?"

Enrique took a deep breath as he leaned over and picked up large sticks of dead mesquite from the ground. "You will remember that many said we could not win over Valdar, either. That he was too strong, too experienced, too evil, too well connected with corrupt officials, and that we were the opposite of all of those things. But look what happened."

Pang knelt down beside Enrique and helped him with the sticks. "We were very determined."

"Yes, and I don't think we ever had a doubt. We had determination but also confidence, and as Father Gaeta said, we had faith. God was on our side."

"I do not doubt this," Pang said, "but it was blind faith. Now, I am not so sure."

Enrique stood, a bundle of sticks cradled in both arms, and he looked directly at his friend. "You understand . . . now, we know exactly what we are doing."

Pang nodded. "Yes, and I wish we didn't."

Once Sosa was out of the cell he was quick to order his men to regroup and get organized. He abhorred any act of confusion, and quickly ordered his guards to retreat to the artillery storage for new guns and bandoleers. There was indeed a mess of empty guns and ammunition all over the tile floors of the cell block and hallways, but it was a waste of good time and men to give it any attention, and a cleanup job better suited for the youth in his employ — the eight-, ten-, twelve-year-old boys in full uniform that roamed the building, polishing his shoes, fetching his laundry, lighting his cigars, or simply delivering messages to people in town. One of their duties was cleaning guns for the guards and organizing the stores of weapons and ammunition. So cleaning up the mess was a good job for these young loyalists, and it was an easy assignment that they handled quickly and efficiently.

Regardless of the orders, Rodríguez retrieved his own pistol and summoned a reloaded of ammunition from a young boy named Ortega. The lad was quick to assist the colonel, and as quick as the cylinder was loaded and shut, Sosa extended his hand toward Rodríguez.

"You mind if I borrow your pistol?" Sosa asked.

Though a bit surprised, Rodríguez obliged his *jefe* and handed him the gun.

Sosa turned and took three steps toward Rufino, whose eyes widened as Sosa lifted his arm and aimed the gun directly at him. The blast deafened the air around them, and the direct shot into Rufino's heart sent him flying backward. Once he hit the floor his last breath of air wheezed through his mouth. No one moved and in contrast to the loud gunshot the air was now haunting and quiet.

Sosa handed the smoking gun back to Rodríguez and paid Rufino no mind. His focus now was on the men that caused this fracas, and since he knew where they were going, he knew exactly what to do to stop them.

"Colonel Rodríguez," Sosa said, walking back into the hallway and toward his office.

The officer gave one last look at the lifeless Rufino then came to quick attention, walking swiftly to catch up. *"Si, patrón?"*

Sosa stepped into his office, put a fresh cigar in his mouth and Rodríguez was quick to supply a match to light it. After several puffs and a fiery ember at the end, Sosa walked to a window behind his desk and looked out into the town. He removed the cigar and squinted through the thick haze of smoke. "Isidro . . . de la Rosa. Do we need him?"

Rodríguez thought for a moment. "He is an expert cook. He has prepared all of our menus and trained all of our chefs. *Si,* he is very valuable."

"Very well, then. That boy . . . Ortega. He is reliable?"

"*Si, patrón.* He knows the city very well,

and everyone knows he works for you."

"Bien." Sosa sat down at his desk and began scribbling a note. When finished he folded the paper twice, and then added his red wax seal. He handed the note to Rodríguez. "Send Ortega out to *Casa del Norte* with this note. It is to be received only by Morales, and no one else."

"Si, patrón."

"Now . . . these men they call *'El Trio'* . . . they are a cunning bunch, indeed. But they are obviously afraid of bullets. Organize a brigade of twenty of our best men. Have them double up on their bandoleers. And I want them all carrying pistols."

"Si, patrón."

"And since we no longer have the services of Rufino, I want you to find Chavón . . . tell him he is now promoted to my driver and body guard. Get him here quickly. That is all."

"Si, patrón." Rodríguez offered a salute but Sosa paid him no mind nor offered a salute in return. After the colonel left the room, all Sosa cared to do was puff heavily on his cigar and blow smoke rings toward the ceiling. He hated defeat as much as he hated anything, but such a situation gave him a profound sense of confidence and power, to retrieve his army of men, his special weap-

ons, and he would exercise all that he had.

It was a calm, comfortable evening, with a light breeze that in only a couple hours would give way to dusk and a chill that would force them to don their jackets. Rodríguez informed Sosa that they would barely have enough time to track them before dark, but Sosa was confident in their circumstances.

"If we waste no time," Sosa said, before taking a deep drag on a fresh cigar, "then it will be perfect."

Rodríguez sent two men — his best trackers — in front of them a good fifty meters. Sosa rode in the middle between Rodríguez and Chavón, who was now fully uniformed, and like the eighteen men in two columns behind them, he wore a pistol at his side, double bandoleers across his chest, and a Winchester rifle in its scabbard. Sosa was proud of how well his militia was armed, and none of it was easy to get. Sure, he could buy the rifles and ammunition the traditional way, from the arms companies themselves, but with a little more effort, he could buy it all for half the price from a smuggler, who bought them from a rogue soldier of the U.S. Army. They still came via ship in the Sea of Cortez, from Puerto

Peñasco to Bahía Kino, but not on a typical freighter. Sosa sent six men, a wagon and mule team to meet the smugglers and pick up the shipments, and so far they had all been successful transactions. Many times Rodríguez had suggested they follow them back to their source, or simply rob the boat, but Sosa would not hear of it.

"It is not our business," Sosa had said. "If we do that, then we lose our source for future purchases, and they are not so easy to come by. No, we should not be so greedy."

But Rodríguez would not get the idea out of his mind, and truly wanted to impress his *jefe* and make a name for himself. He had three men follow the ship back to the source, several kilometers north of San Felipe, and then by horseback to San Luis, where they met up with the original source, who was a man discharged from the recently abandoned Fort Yuma. From there it was not known how he obtained the guns and ammunition, but there was speculation that he stole it from the rail cars on the Southern Pacific. The three men reported this back to Rodríguez, who went to Sosa with the idea of creating their own smuggling operation in order to grow a larger supply of arms at an even lower cost. To show Sosa how easy it was, the men brought back two crates of Model 1873 Winchester carbines, with scores of ammo boxes full of .44-40 cartridges. The presentation to Sosa, however, didn't go as well as they had thought. On a sunny day on a busy street, Sosa took the three men and stood them against a wall, their hands tied behind their backs, and had them executed with the rifles they stole. For two days he hung their bodies by the neck from telegraph poles, with parchment signs pinned to the front of their bloody tunics that read, *"¡Traidores!"*

Colonel Rodríguez feared for his own life, but Sosa gave him a pardon since it was apparent the men acted outside of his orders, that they were only there on reconnaissance. As part of his pardon he was ordered to forget the idea of creating his own smuggling business, however, he was to use the weapons they "collected" to create a special brigade of well-armed soldiers, hence the twenty men with them now. While most of his militia carried single-shot, bolt-action rifles, the most athletic men, the best shots, were given the Winchesters, and they wore a special red and white arm band, which designated that these men were part of Sosa's elite. Though there were over fifty of them, they were all ranked by the level of their skills in hand-to-hand fighting and marksmanship. The five highest skilled were held in reserve and in constant training, with the top-ranked fighter to serve as Sosa's personal body guard. Rufino was number one, but that ranking now belonged to Chavón.

The elite were also armed with a Colt .45 revolver — gunmetal blue with ivory grips and black leather cartridge belts and holsters. No other officer in Sosa's militia was rewarded with such luxuries. Many of them were lucky to have a knife. The top five Sosa knew by name, and he entertained them weekly with a special dinner in their honor, where he rewarded them with wine and a night with a beautiful woman — the best of Sosa's own *puntaría.* Now that Rufino was "removed" from his position, Sosa was introduced to the new "number five" and he now knew him by his name. The rest of the elite fighters were mere numbers, and that's how Sosa referred to them when he and Rodríguez discussed their tactical maneuvers.

One of the trackers turned back and rode up to his leaders. Rodríguez held up a hand and the columns of men stopped.

"We've tracked them into the foothills, *patrón,*" the tracker said, pointing a finger toward a faint plume of smoke rising from the scrub.

Sosa drew a slight grin as he bit into his cigar. "Let's surround them, but keep back a good hundred meters. When it is dark, we will encroach upon the camp. Colonel, I want you to have numbers six through twelve to encircle and move into the camp first, and have them backed up by thirteen through twenty. Once *'El Trio'* are restrained, then you and I will ride in with Chavón to start their trial."

"Si, patrón," Rodríguez said, and then immediately organized the men as Sosa had requested.

And that's how it began. When darkness came upon the landscape, the six men encircled the faint glow of the campfire then crept upon the edge of the camp, got down on one knee and aimed their rifles at the three bedrolls. Once he ascertained that they had secured the camp, number six looked back and signaled with a whistle to Rodríguez. Closely guarded by the other men, dismounted and crouching beside their horses, Rodríguez, Sosa, and Chavón rode slowly toward the campfire carefully observing the mounds of bedding. At that moment one of the men ran up to them and spoke softly. *"Patrón, no hay caballos."*

Sosa studied the bedrolls carefully, then looked at Chavón and nodded. His number one dismounted from his horse, pulled his pistol from its holster, and treaded lightly and slowly into the camp. He was a bull of a man compared to most Mexican men. Six-foot, six inches tall, broad shoulders, and an intimidating pocked face that surrounded a thick, black mustache. He walked lightly around each bedroll, intent and focused, pointing his gun over the cotton blankets that completely covered whoever was under them. He listened carefully for a few seconds, and then studied the fire that had burned down to almost nothing but smoking ash. He leaned over and jerked a blanket away to find nothing but lumps of sticks and scrub branches. He ran quickly to the other two bedrolls only to reveal the same, and all he could do was look alarmingly at Sosa.

"Such a clever trick," Sosa said. "Mount up. Now we go to *Casa del Norte.*"

Casa del Norte was not a large building in itself — an adobe structure with a flat roof and jutting, round wooden *vigas* — but the courtyard outside, with many tables and chairs, some under a *ramada,* covered an area three times as large as the building.

Candles and kerosene lanterns lit the area under the *ramada,* and most of the tables were occupied with hungry patrons, and roaming throughout were men with guitars singing old Mexican ballads.

They had been watching the *restaurante* for two hours, from the sunset shade of a grove of paloverde, eighty meters from the courtyard. The only activity that seemed odd to the business of a *restaurante* was when a boy of about twelve, dressed like one of Sosa's *policía,* came riding in on a horse, in a blasted hurry, and quickly dismounted and ran through the courtyard, weaving through the tables, almost knocking down one of the guitar players, and through the doorway of the main building. The three men looked at each other, each realizing that this was indeed an odd circumstance.

"A courier you think?" Pang asked. "For Sosa?"

A tingling sensation took over Enrique's stomach. Could he really be this close to his *abuelo*? It had been so long since the death of his parents at the hands of Valdar, almost eight years, and two more since his grandfather had left for El Paso. So much had happened. So many days he thought about his grandfather and his welfare, and so many nights he had dreamed of the very moment when they saw each other again. Could this truly be that moment? Enrique knew that it was not healthy to only wish for such moments, but he could not help it. It was especially not healthy now, however, when it might be necessary to take action against anyone inside the *restaurante* who would interfere with Enrique rescuing his *abuelo.*

Enrique looked directly at Sereno. "It is not good for us to be together. Let's split up. Sereno, you go two hundred meters further down the road, and stay close and watch for any more of Sosa's *policía.* Pang, you stay here and keep a careful eye on the *restaurante* and Sereno will come to you if he sees any arriving trouble. It is very important that we do not cause trouble here, because it could only make things worse for us, and *mi abuelo,* if he is here. So at the first sign of complications, we all meet back here. *Entiendes?*"

Sereno nodded.

"Yes, I understand," Pang said. "What are you going to do?"

Enrique took a deep breath and gave a hard look at the *restaurante. "Tengo hambre."*

Pang nodded and put a hand on Enrique's

shoulder. "You have had this hunger for many years, my friend."

Enrique walked back to his horse and rode in to the *Casa del Norte* like a normal, hungry customer. Before he sat down he removed his sombrero and hung it on an empty chair beside him, and then did the same with his bolero jacket. He combed his fingers through his hair and studied the patrons around him, who paid him no mind, and they were mostly men, some only drinking, others digging in to a stack of steaming corn tortillas, vegetables, and a meat, shredded in a peculiar way and topped with a salsa that looked familiar.

The first to meet Enrique was one of the guitar players, who Enrique shooed away with a shake of his index finger. Though he understood that these musicians were there to make a living, compensated by tips from the patrons, Enrique was not in the mood for music. He needed to concentrate.

A waiter, dressed nicely and wearing a white waist apron, black hair slicked with a tonic and neatly parted, walked up to Enrique's table smiling. *"Buenas noches, señor."*

"Buenas noches," Enrique replied. He nodded to the table on his left. "That dish

there, is that lamb?"

"Si, señor," The waiter said. *"Fajitas de cordero."*

"I will have that, please. *Y una cerveza.*"

"Si, señor. Dos pesos, por favor."

He looked up at the waiter, wearing a toothy smile from ear to ear. Enrique reached into his vest pocket and pulled out a small leather pouch, and he dumped out three pesos onto the table, and then slid them across to the waiter. The waiter quickly scooped them into his hands and walked just as quickly to a curtain-covered doorway of the adobe. In less than two minutes the waiter came back through the curtain with a stone mug and set it in front of Enrique.

An old, gray haired woman, swarthy face wrinkled by years in the sun, short and poorly postured, wearing a long dress, brown shawl and a scarf around her neck, shuffled up to Enrique carrying a basket full of green apples. None of these people were employees of the *restaurante,* this Enrique knew. It was very customary in Mexico for street vendors to go wherever the people were to make a living pawning their goods. This old woman was no different than the men with guitars, only she wore the appearance of age and poverty.

"Manzanas, señor," the old woman said.

"Muy fresco."

Enrique looked inside the basket, lined with a cloth, at the speckled and badly bruised apples.

"Cuánto?" Enrique said.

"Tres por uno peso," the old woman said.

Enrique sorted through the apples and picked out the best three, then retrieved a peso for the woman.

"Gracias," the woman said as she turned slowly and shuffled her feet toward the next table.

Enrique put the apples in the pockets of his jacket, then, thinking it to be a good time to look around, left his sombrero and jacket on the chair and grabbed the mug of beer. He wove his way through the tables, nodding politely at anyone who cared enough to pay him any mind, and then found his way to the doorway. Since it was covered by a brown curtain he stepped slightly to the right side, stuck one of his hands between the curtain and doorway and parted it slightly. It was very dark inside, save a few dimly lit tables from candles and lanterns on the wall near them, and the bar, where a bartender stood working with his back to the doorway. There was a hallway that led to other rooms in the back, but it was dark and he could not see any further than its entrance. It seemed very quiet, and the few patrons that were inside sat alone and drank in peace. Enrique was startled by the sudden presence of the waiter who came through the curtain. The waiter was somewhat startled as well.

"Oh, *señor . . . con permiso,*" the waiter said. He held a tray of steaming food. "Your meal, it is ready."

Enrique walked back to his table and sat down, and the waiter set the tray on the table, efficiently placing all of the dishes in front of Enrique. Besides the platter of shredded lamb, accompanied by sliced avocado and cooked cactus, there was a plate of steaming corn tortillas, and three small saucers, one with diced tomatoes, one with chopped white onions, and the other with chilies.

"Will there be anything else?" the waiter asked. *"Más cerveza?"*

Enrique handed the waiter his mug. *"Si, por favor."*

As the waiter walked away with the mug, Enrique inspected the food carefully. It was way too familiar, much like a dish that his mother used to cook for his family. Not so much the cactus and avocado, which were common all over Mexico, or even the lamb, which was also common. But how it was prepared, and the sauce on the meat was unique. Such memories often depressed Enrique, but this was much more real — dizzying and haunting. He grabbed a warm tortilla and with a fork placed some of the lamb on the tortilla, topping it with a few onions and tomatoes. He waved it under his nose and closed his eyes. Yes, this was no common meal. When he opened his eyes he looked down at the tortilla and took a deep breath, then folded it and took a large bite. The taste was even more evocative than the sight or smell. It was as if he had gone back in time to his mother's table, and to the many recipes that were passed down to her by her family. Yes, her father's family. *La familia de Isidro Jesus de la Rosa.*

When the waiter returned with Enrique's mug of beer, he greeted him again with a friendly smile. "How is your food, *señor*?"

Enrique chewed slowly and nodded. After he swallowed, he looked over the entire spread. "This is magnificent. Many compliments to the cook. Is there any way I could meet her? I would like to compliment her personally."

The waiter lost his congenial smile and turned his head slowly toward the doorway. "I am sorry, but the cook has just left. But I will be sure to thank him for you."

"Him?"

"Si . . . Señor de la Rosa."

The tingle already inside Enrique's stomach was intensified at the sound of his grandfather's name. Along with the taste of spicy lamb on his tongue, he sought out the guitar player that he'd already rejected. The musician walked swiftly to Enrique's table, and Enrique laid out two pesos and slid them to the edge. The musician swiped them into his hand and tucked them into his trousers.

"Si, señor," the musician said. "Can I play something special for you?"

Enrique nodded and gazed in thought out into the courtyard. "*Si.* Do you know any old ballads from the mother country?"

"España, señor?"

"Si, cante flamenco?" The musician brought the guitar to his abdomen and began playing, a song that quickly took him away to the pleasurable days of his youth, to the village south of Tucson and north of Tumacácori, where the people would gather, the women would cook, the guitarists would play, and many would dance. Before Enrique could get too caught up in the song, the guitarist slowed and eventually stopped, as he was interrupted by a galloping horse riding up to the courtyard. Enrique looked

to find Sereno riding up. The watchman slowed the horse, and then turned back toward the grove of paloverde where Pang hid, also on the lookout. Enrique thanked the guitarist, shoved the remainder of the taco into his mouth, and then grabbed his jacket and sombrero, walked swiftly to his horse, mounted, and kicked it to a lope. It was painful to know that he had just missed his grandfather, but even more painful to realize that Sosa surely had him removed, but to where might be the most challenging mystery of all. *The boy.* Enrique thought. *The young messenger. It is him we must find.*

CHAPTER FOUR

Sure enough, Sereno had spotted Sosa and several of his men riding the road toward *Casa del Norte.* The three men watched them ride in, the two columns of uniformed soldiers, armed to the teeth, which told Enrique all he needed to know that his plan not to confront them was a good one. There would be a better time, and besides, his grandfather had been moved. To where, that was the question now.

Enrique did not like to intrude on anyone so late, but he was sure Constanza Ramírez would understand, and would be interested in what Sosa had done. It was Jose Flores who answered the door, to one of the Ramírez guards informing him that *"El Trio"* was here to see Señora Ramírez. Jose hesitated, but when Señora Ramírez walked up from behind him, she stepped in front of him and invited them inside. She was dressed in a maroon velour robe over a white nightgown, her hair, which was usually up in a bun, was now loose and long over her shoulders.

"*Con permiso,* Señora Ramírez," Enrique said.

"You do not have to excuse yourself," she answered. She cradled his arm and looked at Pang and Sereno. "And this is the rest of *El Trio*?"

"Well, these are my friends," Enrique said. "But this name, *El Trio* —"

"You must come inside. Are you hungry? Let us fix you something to eat. And I am sure you are all very tired. We have plenty of beds here at the *Hacienda de Ramírez.* My late husband," she said, then paused to make the cross over her chest, ". . . he would entertain many guests. Businessmen, diplomats. People from all over the world." She grabbed both of Enrique's hands and looked softly into his eyes. "But you, we have never made host to a legend."

"Oh, but *señora . . .*"

"Jose!" she shouted. "Take these men to the dining room and serve them a good meal. Get them a bottle of our best sangria. I will get dressed and join you all shortly."

Before Enrique could get in a word, she was gone. He supposed that was the way it was with Señora Ramírez. She was used to being in charge, and having her way, especially now that her husband had passed. But that did not bother Enrique. He felt safe, for him and his friends, at least for the night. It would give them a chance to think about their situation, gather information, and at the same time become allies with Señora Ramírez.

The dining table, which was inside a large room, surrounded by adobe walls and lit by a crystal chandelier, was made of oak, stained dark, and covered with a lace tablecloth. The chairs, and there were twelve of them — five on each side and one on each end — were high backed and upholstered with black leather. Jose sat them next to the end, leaving the end chair open for Señora Ramírez's return. And when she did return, she wore a brown dress, her shoulders covered with a crème colored shawl, and her graying hair back up in a bun. She received proper introductions to each of the men, and her ambition was to see that the men were properly fed.

Along with the sangria, they were served a platter of *sopaipillas,* with honey, as an appetizer, and moments later a tomato-based rice with thick strips of *pollo,* and squash on the side. It was a tasty meal, and they were all very grateful.

After they filled Señora Ramírez in on the happenings of the day, and she was particularly interested in how Enrique escaped from Sosa's jail, she wanted to know more about the legend of *El Trio.* This made Enrique blush a bit, but he did think it was a good time to clear up the confusion about the number. But that did not seem to interest Constanza. She was more interested in the story of how they defeated Antonio Valdar. It was a lengthy story, and Enrique did not want to carry on through the night with it, so he gave her a quick summary. He had her undivided attention.

"I must say," Constanza said, "that is very impressive. These legends, they are always glorified and made to be more than they are, but that is good for the legend. It does not matter what is true in the beginning, or the middle, but in the end it is all the same."

"I see your point," Enrique said.

Constanza took a sip of her wine, then nodded at Enrique. "It has been fairly quiet the past few days, since Sosa's attention has been on you. But I am not naïve. I know that it is only a matter of time before he makes another move. His intention is to own this plantation, and the people who work here. Which will be over my dead body."

"Well, it is my commitment to you to see to it that that does not happen."

Constanza reached across the table and grabbed Enrique's hand. "Consider this your home. You and your friends."

"But I want to make it clear, that I also intend to find my grandfather. If I do, however, that does not mean it is the end of it."

"I believe you. How can I help?"

"I need to find out where they took my grandfather, but I know I cannot go around asking questions without making matters worse for me, and for all of us. I think it best to let things cool down and get to know the people of your *hacienda,* of the town, make new friends, and eventually the information we need may come to us without looking."

Constanza offered a slight smile. "You are a very wise young man."

"I noticed that there are young boys working for Sosa."

Constanza scowled and slammed a fist on the table. "They are easily influenced by his wealth and power! Yet they are too young to know he is only using them to get what he wants. They think he cares for them, but they are wrong!"

"Somehow, we need to reach them. This

may be an answer to getting to the center of Sosa's influence."

"But I do not think it is good to put their lives in any more danger."

"I agree, but I am more concerned about getting them away from Sosa, and back to their families where they belong. It is a better direction for them, don't you think?"

Constanza smiled. "I do." She raised her glass of wine. "To all of you, and to us," she said. *"Salud!"*

They all raised their glasses as well and, save Sereno, repeated the good cheer in unison.

Constanza immediately called for Jose. "Jose will show you to your room, and have our stableman take care of your horses."

Enrique glanced at Sereno, then back at Constanza. "*Señora,* I hope you will not be offended if my amigo, Sereno, does not sleep inside. He has never been much for a feather mattress."

Constanza wrinkled her brow. "Well, where will he sleep?"

Enrique grinned. "I would not worry. Trust that he will be content in taking care of himself."

"Very well then," she said, as she rose from her chair, then offered a slight bow. "It is late. *Buenas noches* to you all."

■ ■ ■ ■

The *Casa del Norte* never closed. In fact, its busiest time was at two and three in the morning. Sosa's elite were relieved from duty, and they all scattered amongst the tables, tequila was served by the bottle, the guitar players all joined together, and the women — the women from the rooms inside — were now among them in the courtyard and under the *ramada,* sitting on their laps and joining in on the music and tequila.

Sosa, however, was inside the adobe, in a special room that was reserved for him. He sat at a desk, one similar to his desk in his office in Hermosillo, and in the chairs in front of him, Roberto Morales, who was the proprietor of *Casa del Norte,* and one of the waiters. Morales, like Sosa, smoked a thick cigar, and a whirling fog surrounded them. He sat with his legs crossed, and his hair was parted neatly and slicked with oil, and he wore a broad, waxed mustache and a handsome gray tweed coat with a silk burgundy cravat tie. Not far from the desk was a walnut poster bed, covered in the finest white linen, but ultimately decorated by Guadalupe Rojas, who lay on her side and up on one elbow, in a red velvet dress that Sosa had imported from Paris. Her raven hair draped over her shoulders and across the coffee colored skin of her bosom, and her curvy hips and thighs were accented by the way she bent one knee and lay one leg over the other.

Sosa paid her a passing glance as he leaned back in his chair and exhaled a large plume of cigar smoke.

Morales held out his hand and tapped off a bit of cigar ash. "As far as we could tell, he was here alone, until the rider came in."

"What did he look like?"

Morales looked at the waiter, who nervously answered the question. "He looked like an Indian, *patrón.* With long hair and a head band. Like an Apache."

Sosa squinted through the haze of smoke. "And the man that you were serving, he left and joined him?"

"*Sí.* He did not finish his food. When he saw the rider come in, he jumped up and left very quickly."

Sosa, his cigar between two fingers, waved it around and looked upward as he pondered the next question. He finally nodded. "This man, did he ask you any questions . . . questions not related to normal business?"

"Not really, *patrón.* He did ask to meet

the cook, but that was because he was very impressed with his meal."

Sosa's chin dropped and he shared a glance with Morales. "And . . . the cook, he was already gone?"

"Si, patrón."

Sosa stood from his chair and set his cigar on a tray. He walked around the desk and both Morales and the waiter stood to meet him. Sosa extended a hand and the waiter shook it. Sosa also patted him on the shoulder. "Thank you, for your great service here. You may go."

"Gracias, patrón."

After the waiter left the room Sosa followed Morales to the door, and when there Morales turned to face him.

"So everything is as planned?" Sosa asked.

Morales looked over to the bed, and Guadalupe stared back at him haughtily.

Sosa turned to look at her too, then back at Morales. "Oh, do not worry about her. She is more loyal than you."

"I did just like your note said, and two men escorted Isidro to the Hotel Catedral, where he is secretly under guard until you give us further instructions."

"Muy bien," Sosa said. "So the boy, Ortega, where is he now?"

Morales shrugged. "Outside, in the courtyard . . . with your men I think?"

Sosa nodded and extended his hand. Morales shook it firmly.

"That will be all," Sosa said. "And I do not want to be disturbed."

"Si, patrón."

After Morales left, Sosa locked the door and turned to look at Guadalupe. She grinned seductively, rose slowly to her hands and knees and crawled to the foot of the bed. Sosa walked and met her there. He took off his coat and shoulder holster and hung them on the bed post. Guadalupe stood on her knees and unbuttoned his vest, then shirt, and pushed them over his shoulders to where they fell on the floor. She ran the back of her hand gently down the side of his face, and then the fingertips of both hands down his chest. They never lost eye contact.

He wove the fingers of one hand into her hair and studied it closely. "You are my most loyal, right *mi amor*?"

She leaned forward and kissed his chest indiscriminately, but did not answer. He grabbed a handful of hair on the back of her head and pulled backward. She looked up at him fearfully. *"Si, mi amor. Siempre."*

Sosa laughed out loud and then pressed his lips firmly against hers. He let go of her hair and she embraced him around the neck as they fell backward on the bed. Though it was a minor victory, it was a step toward the kind of success Sosa was used to. And it was a good enough feeling that it prompted the yearning to share the rest of the night with Guadalupe Rojas.

After being shown to his room, Enrique was not quite up to sleeping, and decided to take a walk around the *rancho* in the cool night air. He left his sombrero in the room, but wore his jacket to cut the chill. The lumps in the jacket pockets reminded him that he'd bought the three apples. He pulled one of them out and examined it. *Poor old woman,* he thought. Then again, she may have been better off than most, working around all of those hungry men. Maybe the "poor old woman" display was merely a front for her business? Oh well, if so she had Enrique's respect. The apples, they were not so badly bruised that they couldn't be eaten, but he was still full from his recent meal. He walked into the stable, not only to check on his horse, but also to inspect the belongings in his saddle bags.

He found the bay mare and rubbed a hand down the side of her neck. She was a fine horse, and Enrique had grown quite fond of her. He bought her in Tucson shortly after getting back from El Paso, with the reward money for capturing Valdar. After he, Sereno, and Father Gaeta had sweated for most of the day raising and mounting the new bell into the tower, Father Gaeta convinced Enrique that it was okay to have the money. "It's not a sin to have money, or to earn it," the priest had said. "It is what you do with money that determines your fate with God."

"Then you do not think God would mind if I bought a good horse?"

The priest laughed loudly. "No, my son. In fact, I think God would smile down on you with happiness."

That was all Enrique needed to arouse more interest, and to seek Chas Dutton's help in finding the right one. Horse flesh was not something that Enrique claimed to know anything about. Where he came from, you were lucky to have a burro to walk beside, let alone ride. But Dutton, he was a good judge, and someone he trusted to help him find the best deal.

And he did. Whenever he rode the streets, or visited the ranchos, the bay mare turned a lot of heads. Dutton warned him that he'd arrested many horse thieves, and very few of them stole bad horses, so to be careful with this one.

Enrique walked down the side of the mare and rubbed her across the back. She whickered and shook her head. He found the saddlebags hanging on a hook on the stable wall. He opened one of them and found a white cotton cloth, and took the apples from his pockets and one by one wrapped them in the cloth. When he got to the third apple, he stopped, then walked back to the front of the mare and held it under her nose. She lapped it up quickly and crunched until a frothy juice seeped between her lips.

He gave her one last affectionate rub on the forehead then walked back to the saddlebags, regarded his saddle on a stand nearby, and there he found his bow and quiver. He pulled one of the arrows from the quiver and inspected it, and was comforted by its condition and the fact that he still had possession of any of them. While he was in jail, and his horse was left here, Sereno had found his way to retrieve it so it would be near when he got out. Little did Sereno know that the livery owner, across the street from the jail, was connected to Sosa. But, little did the livery owner know that the bow and arrows, in the days of impressive firearms, were Enrique's weapon of choice.

Just as Enrique was about to put the arrow back in the quiver, he heard a voice. Then he heard it again, the voice of a young woman, and she was yelling.

He stepped out of the stall into the main opening of the stable, and the yelling voice grew louder, and there was now another voice, that of a young boy. Enrique kept walking, until he was outside, and he walked around the adobe wall of the stable to the side of the building where he found the young woman, a shawl wrapped over her head and shoulders, and a boy that Enrique figured to be about ten years old standing holding a rifle. When they both saw him, the boy turned wide-eyed, then stepped slowly backward.

"Is everything okay?" Enrique said.

The boy quickly turned and ran away into the darkness.

The young woman called out to him. "No! Felipe! *Por favor,* Felipe!"

Enrique walked toward the woman and she looked back at him, clutching her shawl closed with both hands.

"I am sorry if I scared him away," Enrique said. "Are you all right?"

The woman bowed her head slightly. "No, I am very afraid."

"Of what?"

"*Mi hermanito.* He is inspired by his older

brother to join up with Arriquibar Sosa. There is no stopping this influence. His own family cannot stop him!"

"His older brother, he is young also?"

"*Sí.* He is only twelve."

"That is very young," Enrique said. "Forgive me. My name is Enrique Osorio. I am a guest of Señora Ramírez."

The young woman lifted her chin, her face nearly smiling. "*Sí,* I have heard of you. You are one of *El Trio,* no?"

Enrique laughed under his breath. "Well, that is what they call us, but we have never gone by that name."

She stepped closer to him and grabbed one of his hands in both of hers. "My name is Emanuela Ortega. I am a teacher here, at the private school for the people of the rancho."

"Ortega?"

"If you could only hear everyone talk. *El Trio,* on our rancho! You are a gift from God!"

"Oh, *señorita . . .*"

"Sosa, he comes to the school uninvited, and walks around the room inspecting the boys, and before he leaves, he points at one, makes him stand and says, 'You.'

"The boy, he thinks he is the lucky one. But he is too young to know that he may never live to be a man. This is what happened to my brother, Amado, who was one of the oldest boys in the school. He has been with Sosa for two months now. Every night, my mother, she cries herself to sleep!"

"What about your father?" Enrique asked. "Does he support Sosa?"

A wave of sadness caused Emanuela's face to turn ashen. "Sosa killed my father."

Enrique stood perplexed. "And your brothers . . . they know this?"

"My father worked for Sosa. He died as a sacrifice. A martyr. And that is the way my brothers see it. But only those of us with courage, and our eyes open wide, know that Sosa uses people only to gain for himself."

"I see. I would like to talk to your brother."

"Oh, Señor Osorio, that would be wonderful! I would be forever in your debt."

Enrique held up a hand. "Well, I would wait until I talk to him. You will not think so if I make things worse for him."

"You could not make things any worse," Emanuela said. "As of now there is no hope. At least with you, a legend, a hero, making an effort . . . there is hope!"

Enrique nodded and smiled. "I will try."

Emanuela's eyes widened. "And maybe you could come to the school! Yes, that is a wonderful idea!"

"To the school?"

"Yes, don't you see? You are a legend. The children, they talk about *El Trio* as much as they do Sosa! You can help them to see the good in life, the loyalty of family, and not the way of the corrupt ways of a government."

Enrique took a deep breath and let it out slowly. "But we must be careful. It will cause much trouble between the school and Sosa. As I have learned, he will stop at nothing to win. I don't want innocent women and children to get hurt."

"Don't you see? We have no future with Sosa. Only greed and corruption. We need our families back. We need our freedom . . . to live our own lives without fear."

Enrique studied the hopeful expression on Emanuela's face. "Okay, I will try."

Her smile could have lit up the night, and her forceful embrace not only took Enrique by surprise, but he suddenly realized that he had never had a woman so beautiful hold him the way she did. It was warm and comfortable, strangely perfect, and the sweet smell of her hair underneath his chin gave him a calm, peaceful feeling.

She let go slowly, grabbed both of his hands and looked softly up into his eyes. There was no doubt in Enrique's mind that there could not be a more perfect face.

"*Buenas noches,* Señor Osorio."

"There is no need to be so formal. *Por favor,* call me Enrique."

Emanuela shook her head. "I could not —"

Enrique put his index finger over her mouth. *"Si,* you can. *Buenas noches."*

Chapter Five

It was a short night for all of them, from the moment the roosters started crowing, until the servants of the *hacienda* knocked on the doors to their rooms, walked inside to the windows and opened the wooden shutters letting the blinding sunshine into their rooms. Enrique was informed that breakfast was about to be served in the main dining room, a place they were familiar with. After splashing his face with cool water from the wash bowl, he quickly dressed and went to find Sereno. He didn't waste any time looking for him, but instead walked outside, near the stable, and whistled like a desert bird that no one had ever heard but Enrique and Sereno. Sure enough, in less than a minute, Sereno seemed to come out of nowhere, dressed and ready. Enrique never failed to be impressed at how Sereno was *always* dressed and ready.

Pang also found a spot in an orange grove

for his routine morning meditation, which caught the attention of the many field workers who watched him stretch, kick, and breathe while they began their workday.

Following a breakfast of fresh baked bread, melon, mandarins, and eggs mixed with peppers, onions, and tomatoes, Enrique requested a meeting with Constanza and her foremen. He made a special request to include whoever was in charge of the many guards that stood post in particular areas around the *hacienda,* and made it clear that this meeting only include people that she absolutely trusted, without any doubt.

A server walked around the table pouring each of them coffee. Constanza waited for him to finish and when the nicely dressed old man started to leave the room, she grabbed his arm to stop him. "Arturo, I need you to have Fernando and Jose come here to the dining room immediately."

The servant nodded. *"Si, señora."*

Within minutes Jose was seated next to Constanza and across from Enrique, and Fernando Jiménez, who was introduced as her ranch foreman, sat next to him and across from Pang.

"Fernando is in charge of anything outside of the *hacienda,*" Constanza said. "Which not only includes the field and stable workers, but also the hiring of our security. Jose, who you already know, oversees all of our personnel inside the *hacienda,* but he works very closely with Fernando. They both report directly to me."

Constanza expressed her understanding of Enrique's concern for secrecy, and confessed that someone in her employ had to be giving Sosa information, but she could only speculate who it might be.

Enrique nodded and studied the faces of the two *jefes.* "Perhaps it is children?"

Constanza looked solemnly at Enrique. "You see, the people who are working here have a choice. All of them could leave and work for Sosa. Some for better money. They are either here because they hate Sosa and what he stands for, or because they are spies. But children? This I do not understand."

"I spoke to a young woman last night," Enrique said. "*Una maestra,* Emanuela."

"Si," Constanza said. "Emanuela has been a teacher in our school for two years now. But I would never believe her to be a spy."

"No-no," Enrique said. "It's not her I would worry about. It's her students."

After taking a drink from his coffee cup, Jose set it on the table and licked his lips, then shared a concerned glance. "Why do you think this way?" Jose asked.

"It was very late last night, in the alley behind the stable," Enrique said. "She was trying to stop her very own brother from running off, with a rifle in hand, to join up with Sosa. I spoke with her, and she explained how Sosa recruited her students. And then she told me about her other brother, Amado Ortega, who was already working for him. It was him, Amado, who delivered the message for Sosa to *Casa del Norte* to have my grandfather taken away before I found him."

Jose shrugged. "I understand, but the boys are not here, they are with Sosa. How can they be spies?"

"I thought about this, too," Enrique said. "Emanuela explained that they cannot leave and join up with Sosa until he approves — or until they have earned their way in. These boys, they are very impressionable."

Constanza nodded. "Yes, I can see your reasoning. What do you think we should do?"

"It is best not to react, but to watch. I suggest we find someone to watch the children of the school, and see who leaves the rancho, and follow them to where they go. It may take a few days, but when we discover who it is, they will lead us to the vein of communication, and when we cut it off, it is Sosa's time to react."

Constanza looked at Fernando. "What do you think?"

Fernando shook his head. "I think it is a waste of time. Children as spies? No, I do not believe it."

Enrique leaned forward and rested his elbows on the table as he spoke, looking directly at Fernando. "You heard me when I said that the Ortega boy was Sosa's courier. It gives these boys purpose. And the younger boys look up to the older boys. To the boys in that school now, Amado is their idol. That is why his younger brother, Felipe, ran off to join up with Sosa. He looks up to his older brother, who wears a uniform, and works directly with the most powerful man in Sonora. Yes, he is the new recruit."

Jose leaned forward anxiously. "*Si,* I remember now. For many days Felipe was truant. Emanuela complained of it. He would be gone for hours, into Hermosillo, and not return until late in the evening. And many days we would have to run him out of the house, the kitchen, the study, and one day I caught him in the wine cellar drinking wine! He was angry and defiant, and I dragged him yelling and screaming back to his mother. She complained that she could not control him. That it was bad when his father died, but now it was worse since his brother had left."

They all looked at Fernando, who seemed indifferent to anything that had been said.

"Okay," Constanza said. "Fernando, who can we get to watch these children?"

Fernando shrugged. "I am not sure at the moment, but I will think of someone."

"May I make a suggestion?" Enrique said.

"Of course," Constanza replied.

Enrique looked down the table at Sereno. "We have, at your service, the best watchman I have ever known. And . . ." Enrique nodded at Fernando. ". . . this way we can be sure that he is on our side."

Fernando leaned back in his chair and took a deep breath, all the while staring at Enrique, and then looked at Constanza. "*Señora,* there is no need to worry. Our people can be trusted. Besides, if Señor Osorio is right, then it is children that we need to worry about."

Constanza, in deep thought, looked at Fernando a moment, down the table at Sereno, then at Enrique. "I like your idea, Señor Osorio. You are right, this way there is no risk."

Enrique nodded. "Consider it done,

señora."

Fernando glared contemptuously at Enrique.

Constanza continued. "But this is a solution to only one small problem. Once this is stopped, then comes the real storm."

"I agree, but I also believe that from the information we gather, we can learn more about Sosa's intentions."

Constanza put both hands on the table and gnashed her teeth before she spoke. "I know of his intentions! It is to take everything for himself! Not just this ranch, but all of Hermosillo. All of Sonora!"

Enrique reached across and gently held one of Constanza's hands. *"Si, señora.* That is what he wants to achieve. But there are many things he will have to do to get that far. A head-to-head attack will never work against Sosa. That is what he is most prepared to handle. If we quietly work our way in, we can stop it all. *Entiendes?"*

Jose grabbed Constanza's other hand. She looked at both of them and found a slight smile. "Sometimes I forget we are in the presence of greatness. We have *El Trio* on our side."

Enrique wanted to talk more with Constanza, and give her more details of their plans, but he had a greater concern. Once they left the *hacienda* and went to the stable, he pulled Pang and Sereno aside, making sure no one was near or could hear him.

He looked directly at Pang. "Did you notice what I noticed?"

"Yes," Pang said. "Fernando. Something is not right about him."

Enrique put his hands on both hips, took a deep breath and looked up in thought. "It's either one of two things."

"One, he is in with Sosa," Pang said.

"Yes. Or he could just be jealous of our presence. Security is his responsibility, and I am sure he does not like others in charge. And if things fall apart, it could mean losing his job."

Pang nodded. "Which do you think it is?"

Enrique looked at Sereno. "I want you to watch the school closely. Someone has had to take Felipe's place as a messenger. Follow him, and when you find out where he is going, and who he is talking to, then we will make our plans."

Sereno did not hesitate and left the stable.

"We need to keep an eye on Fernando, also," Pang said.

"Yes, do you think you can do it?"

Pang nodded. "I am no secret around

here. People see me and will suspect nothing. I will be discreet."

Enrique smiled and put a hand on his shoulder. "I know you will be."

"What are you going to do?"

"I have to wait for Sereno to return with his information. I know it is dangerous, but I am going to go into town."

"And do what?"

"I need to talk to that boy, Amado Ortega."

Pang's brow wrinkled as he expressed his confusion. "But he knows who you are."

"True. But I have an idea. One that will require some help from *la maestra.*"

It was a bright, sunny day, and Emanuela stood outside the entrance of the adobe school house wearing a black, ankle length, tiered skirt, with a white, broached collared blouse and gray shawl. Her attention was on the children as they played in the yard in front of the school house. The boys acted like Sosa's *policía,* standing in full attention while the tallest and oldest of the boys, Javier, barked orders with his make-believe gun — an extended finger and thumb. The girls were nowhere near, huddled in the shade of a paloverde laughing and sharing secrets. When Emanuela pulled on the rope that rang the bell on top of the school house, the girls were quick to rise and run into the building. The boys, however, paid no attention to the bell, and only to the game they were playing. Or was it a game?

Emanuela marched over to them and stood firmly, pointing toward the door of the school house. "You stop this foolishness now and get back into the school!"

Javier took two steps closer to her, and since he was as tall as Emanuela, he looked fiercely into her eyes. "We do not take orders from you."

Emanuela took a deep breath as she stared back at the boy. "This man, he is ruining you." She scanned the line of boys and made eye contact with all of them. "I am your *maestra,* and if you do not obey me, I will take you to your parents, and this will be settled here and now."

Javier laughed. "*Mi madre?* She is weak." His face grew stern. "And I have no father."

"But you have an uncle," Emanuela said. "Your mother's brother, Jeronimo. I know him, and I know he would not approve of this behavior. If you do not get back in that school right this second, I will get him. It is a promise."

Javier glared angrily, and then cracked a slight grin. "*Vayamos, amigos.* There will be a better time."

Sereno watched it all through a small window from inside the stable. He understood the challenge she was having with the boys, it was obvious. And he was a bit surprised that she was able to lure them back in. She followed them all, but Javier, who flanked the line of boys in front of her, shifted quickly away and ran from the school and into the orange grove. Emanuela yelled for him, but it did no good.

Sereno watched him carefully weave through the trees and around the workers, and ascertained that he was heading into the city. His horse already saddled, Sereno mounted and rode through the doorway and toward the lane next to the orange grove. He kicked it to a lope and eventually he could see the boy run out of the orange grove and into a scrubby wilderness across the road. It was not near as difficult to find his trail as it was to keep up with him, but Sereno was an expert at such a thing. Before long he found himself deep into the heart of Hermosillo, into an alley, and watching Javier run into the back door of a cantina. Sereno rode out of the alley and to the street in front of the cantina. He looked up at the brown letters above the door painted on the white adobe building, and they read: *Cantina de El Manadero.*

Enrique waited patiently near the water well in a stone courtyard near the school, and before long he watched a young girl come out of the building and ring the bell. Within minutes the children exited the building to meet their families in the courtyard, and Enrique stood watching them, but kept a watchful eye on Emanuela. She stood amongst all of them, cheerfully greeting each of them and bidding them farewell. Eventually she saw him, smiled and waved. When the children and families had all dispersed she started walking toward him and he decided to do the same, meeting her near the middle of the courtyard.

"*Buenas tardes,* Señor Osorio," Emanuela said, followed by a tender smile. "It is nice to see you."

Enrique removed his hat. "Likewise, *señorita.*"

"What brings you here?" she asked.

Enrique returned his hat to his head then squinted into the sunlit courtyard and scanned the area. He looked back at the inquiring stare of Emanuela. "I was wondering if you might help me."

She nodded. "*Si,* if I can. How can I help you?"

"How are you with disguises?"

The teacher laughed. "I am afraid I do not understand."

"If I go in town, the way I am now, Sosa's men will recognize me. I need to look different, like a businessman. I want to talk to your brother Amado."

Emanuela's face grew solemn. "This sounds very dangerous, Señor Osorio."

"Every day in this life is dangerous. If we do not try to get through to these young men, it will only get worse."

Emanuela nodded. "Okay, how can I help?"

Pang spent most of the day getting to know the people of *Hacienda de Ramírez.* He started by walking through the orange groves and fields, stirring the curiosity of the people about who this Chinaman was and whether or not it was good to know him. Word had already spread throughout the plantation that he was a member of *El Trio,* and before long, accompanied by his friendly demeanor, he had earned the people's confidence. The workers in the fields reminded Pang of his youth in China, and the people in the rice fields — the broad hats protecting them from the sun, many of them with bare feet. But there was much poverty back home, and this situation seemed much more stable and productive. He took particular notice, however, of the men who rode through the fields on horseback. Supervisors to the workers, no doubt. There weren't many of them, but one was always in sight, and they didn't seem all that interested in Pang. They rarely responded to his greetings in any way, most of them looking away and riding off.

As Pang entered another cotton field, he heard a commotion between one of the supervisors — one they called Jorge — and a worker, and another worker ran to the scene to get involved. As Pang got closer, he acknowledged that the worker was sitting on the ground, and that he was elderly, and the other worker, a young woman, wearing a broad hat, long white dress and faded red apron, was at his side trying to help him to his feet but was getting nowhere.

"What's wrong with him?" Jorge shouted, still on horseback.

"He has been ill, and weak," the young woman said. "He just needs to rest a moment."

The supervisor spat a large stream of tobacco juice then nodded toward them with his chin. “He needs to get off his ass and get to work, or he can leave the plantation now.”

The young woman kept trying to get the old man on his feet, but he labored to breathe and there was not enough she could do to help him.

Jorge turned his horse more broadside, and raised his right arm to reveal a leather quirt coiled in his hand.

Pang walked over to try and help her, but when he knelt down and got a better look at the old man, he could see that this man was in no condition to work.

He looked up at Jorge. “This man needs rest, and a doctor.”

Jorge narrowed his eyes. “Hey *Chino,* why don’t you get out of here and mind your own damned business.”

Pang rose to his feet. “In case you haven’t heard, helping people is my business.”

“You get out of here now or I’ll thrash your ass out of here.”

Pang took three steps closer to the horse. “Sir, have you ever gone to a well for water, but there was no more water?”

“What the hell are you talking about?”

“Thrashing this man will get you no more work, no more than thrashing the bucket would give you more water.”

"How about I just thrash you? That work, *Chino*?"

Pang walked closer, within arm's length of the horse, and the supervisor raised his arm higher and uncoiled the quirt.

Pang held his hand up shoulder high. "Since there is no reasoning with you, how about I dump your *ass* off that horse?"

Before the supervisor could extend his arm any farther, Pang reached a hand under the horse's front legs, causing it to rear, and Jorge fell backward to the ground. In a stir of dust he quickly jumped to his feet, found the quirt he had dropped, and located Pang with a wide-eyed glare.

Pang stood at a ready stance, almost sideways, knees slightly bent, arms raised and hands elongated. Jorge gnashed his teeth and snapped the quirt, which Pang blocked with his left forearm, causing it to wrap around it several times. Before the supervisor could react, Pang pulled on the quirt which jerked the man off his feet and into a sprawling display facedown on the ground.

Pang wasted no time pushing his knee into the man's back and keeping him under control. "How is your *ass* now, sir?"

The man growled and said nothing, and only tried to squirm his way out of the predicament. Pang looked at the young woman, and then nodded toward Jorge's horse standing nearby. "Go get the horse, and I will help you put the old man on it. You can use it to take him home, where he can rest until he is ready to come back to work."

The young woman hesitated, but eventually did what Pang said.

Pang kept his knee pressed firmly into Jorge's back and leaned his head closer to the man's ear. "I will get off of you now, but when I do, you will stand back and not interfere with the woman. *Entiendes jefe?*"

The supervisor continued to breathe strongly in and out his nose, but he quickly nodded. *"Si."*

Pang patted the man on the shoulder. "Very good." He rose up off the man, who followed by slowly rising to his knees, then to his feet. He stood there looking awkwardly at them as Pang and the young woman helped the old man onto the horse.

The young woman glanced at Jorge timidly, and at the same time spoke to Pang, almost in a whisper. "*Señor,* I appreciate your help. But there is no way Fernando will ever let this man return to work. And I will likely be fired for helping him!"

Once the old man was steady in the

saddle, Pang handed the reins to the young woman. "Do not worry. Me and Fernando, we are good friends. I will see to it that all is well for both of you."

The young woman looked back at Pang with an expression of disbelief. *"Gracias, señor,"* she said, and then pulled the horse away and toward the workers' quarters.

Constanza was very generous to loan a gray suit coat and trousers to Enrique, along with a white shirt, gray silk cravat, a dress hat, and no questions asked. She said that Enrique was about the same size as her son, who Sosa had killed, and that he would have been proud to know that a man of *El Trio* wore his clothes to help bring down Sosa. Enrique understood Constanza's pain, and it was a big part of what drove him to help her. He knew what it was like to lose a family.

Since Enrique had never worn clothes such as these, Emanuela helped with the preparations. She slicked his hair with a touch of olive oil, parted and combed it neatly, and after he stepped out from behind the privacy of a dressing screen, wearing everything but the hat, which he held in his hand, he felt as awkward about his appearance as he did her blushing.

"Is something wrong?" he asked.

"No," she said bashfully. *"Eres muy guapo."*

Now Enrique was blushing. "*Gracias, señorita.* I guess that means it is a good disguise?"

She stepped closer to him and smoothed out the lapels of his coat with the palms of her hands, and then ran each of her hands gently across his shoulders. Now only inches from his face, she looked up into his eyes.

He had never been this close to a woman's face. A woman his own age. A woman who made the nerve endings tingle all over his body.

He took a deep breath. "*Señorita,* I am feeling very dizzy."

"Perhaps it is a good dizzy?"

"*Si,* too good, perhaps."

She leaned closer to him. "Would you like to kiss me, Enrique?"

He fidgeted with the hat with both hands, his heart beating a little faster, and he felt the need to take more frequent breaths. "I have a confession to make, *señorita.*"

"*Por favor,* call me Emanuela."

"*Si* . . . Emanuela . . ."

She put both of her hands on his chest. "What is your confession?"

"I — I have never kissed a girl — a woman."

"Never?"

Enrique shook his head nervously, and the deeper he looked into her eyes, the more entranced he became. "What about you?"

"Feeling like this? No, Enrique. Never." She reached down and grabbed both of his hands, causing the hat to fall to the floor, and with both hands in hers she pulled one of them up to her face, where she rubbed the tips of his fingers across her cheek and closed her eyes. He studied her face, every contour, and her lips, and with what little strength he had, he leaned his head forward, now feeling her breath on his chin, closed his eyes and pressed his lips lightly against hers. The dizzy feeling before was nothing compared to now, and his entire body felt locked in place and he was afraid to move, in that he might fall. But he opened his eyes slightly, and saw that hers were still closed, and when he pulled away she opened her eyes and smiled at him, then lay her head sideways against his chest. He reached his arms around her and held her.

She leaned back and looked up at him. "If you ever fall in love with me, you can call me Ema. But only then."

He nodded and smiled and caressed her chin with the knuckle of his index finger. "I should be going."

They both stepped backward but held on to each other's hands.

"Come back to me soon, Enrique."

He nodded and smiled. "I will."

As he stepped away she called quickly to him. "Enrique, wait!"

He stopped and turned to look at her.

She reached down to the floor and picked up his hat. "You cannot forget this."

She walked up to him and put the hat on his head and adjusted it properly. Before he could react, she kissed him quickly on the lips and then turned him and pushed him toward the door. "Go, Enrique. Your work is very important. *Cuidado.*"

After she opened the door and he stepped outside into the daylight, he turned one more time and looked back at her magnetic eyes and intoxicating smile. He tipped his hat and nodded. *"Buenas noches."*

The sun was now low in the western sky, a coolness in the air, and dim shadows of the buildings on the *hacienda* cut out any light that was left of the day. Enrique went to the stable, where a stable worker waited with a horse-drawn carriage prepared as an additional disguise. Many businessmen, Constanza had told him, come into town but they do not ride horseback. Though Enrique had not mastered the use of a harness he had driven a buckboard many times, and felt confident the ease of it would come quickly.

As he was about to board the buggy, the stable worker opened the double doors at the end of the barn, and they were both startled by the sudden appearance of Sereno as he rode in and his horse came to an abrupt halt. Sereno jumped down from the horse and scanned the entire area of the stable, and when he found what he was looking for, he pointed to a plume of smoke that rose from one of the stalls. The stable worker quickly grabbed a bucket and ran for water, and just as Enrique started to run toward the stall, Sereno stopped him and lured him outside the barn.

They both jogged around to the alley and Sereno pointed again, to Javier who stopped for a short moment, stared back wide-eyed at the men, and then ran into the shadows of the evening.

Sereno started to run after him, but Enrique grabbed hold of his arm and stopped him. "Let him go."

They both ran back into the barn and helped the stable worker put out the fire. While he poured a bucket of water at the base of the flames, Sereno found a blanket and beat the rest of it out, while burying his nose and mouth into the bend of his elbow. The stable worker grabbed a pitchfork and used it as a rake to drag the unburned straw away from the fire. In less then a minute they had the fire out and reduced to a small pile of smoldering ash.

Enrique walked with Sereno back outside where he could get some fresh air. Once recovered and not breathing so heavily, Sereno looked Enrique up and down, noticeably perplexed by his attire.

Enrique understood his confusion. "It is part of a plan."

Sereno nodded and shrugged it off, and then he started communicating with Enrique in sign language. Though he pretty much already knew, Enrique quickly understood that Javier was sent here to burn the barn, an initiation into the world of Arriquibar Sosa, and part of the plot to force Constanza Ramírez to sell out. Sereno also informed Enrique that the *Cantina de El Manadero* was a leisurely hangout for Sosa and his top *policía,* and the boys were constantly running in and out of the cantina with courier messages.

Enrique put a hand on Sereno's shoulder. "Are you okay?"

He nodded while taking in a deep breath.

Enrique smiled. "You did good. Now get some rest."

Chapter Six

The streets of Hermosillo were now under complete darkness, save the casting glow from doors and windows, or the scarce gaslights that offered a faint glow on what few pedestrians walked the streets or gathered outside the buildings. Enrique drove the buggy through the dirt and cobblestone streets of the town drawing very little attention, and though he was pleased with his disguise, he was glad that the black of the night helped him all that much more.

Once he located *Cantina de El Manadero* he stopped across the street and lit a *cigarillo,* then watched for a moment, and listened to the noise inside. The mariachi music from inside was loud enough that drunken pedestrians sang and danced, and occasionally a uniformed *policía* would laugh and join in. The moment a young boy dressed in a khaki uniform came running down the street and into the cantina, Enrique knew he had found the right place. He took one last drag off the *cigarillo* then flicked it into the street, snapped the reins and drove away. A good eighty kilometers down the same street he found a livery where he could leave the horse and buggy, not knowing how long he would be, or how safe it would be to leave it in the street. Then again, it was Sosa's town. How safe was anywhere in Hermosillo?

He found his way back to the cantina and walked through the disorderly fiesta taking place outside the front door. Once he was through the batwing doors, he stood and scanned the large room, loud with music and drunken, singing men, with as many women sitting on their laps or roaming about looking for business. Many of the men held bottles of wine or tequila while others gulped beer from stone mugs. No one acknowledged him, and he started to walk slowly amongst the crowd seeking an empty chair or table, and eventually found one against the wall where there was very little light. Eventually a rather voluptuous *señorita* came to his table, rubbed her knee against his and a finger under his chin.

"Hola, guapo," the woman said seductively.

Enrique was afraid to lift his head too high.

"What can I get for you?"

"I will have a beer."

She rubbed the same finger gently down the side of his face. *"Solo una cerveza, guapo?"*

"Yes, that is all."

Along with a bit of disappointment on her face, the woman walked away from the table and wove her way through the crowd. Enrique scanned the room again, then noticed a stairway along the wall straight ahead of him, that led to a balcony and stretched across the entire width of the room. Two armed guards, who appeared to be on duty and not part of the fiesta, stood at the foot of the stairs. Whenever someone tried to walk up the stairs, many were rejected, some by force, and others were let through. Enrique noticed three other armed guards behind the rail on top, spaced evenly across the expanse of the balcony. The balcony wasn't very deep, maybe three or four feet, Enrique thought, with five doors on the opposite wall that led to private rooms. Since the boys or Sosa or any of his top guards were nowhere to be found, Enrique assumed they were all in those highly guarded rooms.

What a treat it must be, Enrique thought, and a glowing feeling for those young boys to be able to pass the guards and enter the rooms when so many grown men couldn't. He was sure that this was a big part of what lured them to the excitement of crime and corruption — what gave them a sense of adventure that they could not get at the *Hacienda de Ramírez.*

The guards let one of the men through and he walked up the stairway, knocked on the center door, and eventually it was opened by an elegant woman wearing a red silk dress, a garment of high fashion very seldom seen in Mexico, let alone Hermosillo. She let the man in, and before she shut the door, Sosa walked through, dressed in his trademark white pants and vest, a cigar clenched in his teeth, and rested his hands on the balcony rail. Enrique lowered his head slightly, hoping his hat brim would shadow his face, but just enough that he could still look up and see Sosa. The *patrón* looked over the entire floor of happy men, as if he were inventorying all of them, but Enrique knew that this was merely a man looking over his kingdom, as if he were God Himself.

A sudden nervous feeling overcame Enrique when Sosa looked directly at him and removed the cigar from his mouth. He stared at him a short moment them summoned the guard closest to him. The man came quickly, and Sosa pointed with his cigar toward Enrique and spoke. The guard looked toward Enrique and shrugged, then Sosa returned the cigar to his mouth and put his hands back on the rail. He looked at Enrique only a few seconds longer before he was interrupted by the woman in the red silk dress. At that very instant a boy in uniform came out through the door and Sosa rubbed him on the head then shooed him away.

The boy scurried across the balcony and down the stairs, and when he got into the crowd Enrique immediately recognized him as Felipe. He watched the boy all the way to the door, and by that time the *señorita* had arrived with Enrique's beer. He stood without acknowledging her but tossed three pesos out onto the table and then walked quickly to the door. When he got to the door, he stopped only for a short moment and looked back toward the balcony, and was haunted to see Sosa once again standing there, hands on his hips, smoldering cigar in his mouth, looking right at him.

Though it was difficult to see in the dark street, Enrique caught a glimpse of the khaki uniform of the running boy and walked swiftly in that direction. He followed him down five city blocks and across three different streets, until he walked into an area of many small wooden and adobe houses, and stopped and knocked on the door of one.

Enrique was afraid to get too close to someone's personal dwelling, so he hid nearly a block away, along side a building where he could peek around and keep an eye on Felipe. The small adobe appeared to be some sort of business but was shut down for the evening, therefore Enrique felt safer and out of view.

The door in front of Felipe opened and his face was lit by the faint light from inside the house. A bare-chested man, his suspenders hanging loose at his hips, appeared in front of Felipe, acknowledging the youngster only briefly before looking up and down the street. Felipe handed the man a folded paper document, then turned quickly and ran back in the direction from which he came. Enrique took a step back and prepared for the moment when the boy ran past him, and that was when he caught a glimpse of light behind him and the pungent smell of sulfur.

He turned quickly to find a uniformed *policía* lighting a cigar with a match, and also acknowledged two men behind him, both wearing wide sombreros and street clothes; each held rifles, and double bandoleers crossed their chests.

The policeman removed the smoking cigar from his mouth and smiled widely. "*Hola, señor.* Can I help you with something?"

Enrique stood nervously and took a deep breath. "I am sorry if I alarmed you. I feel as though I am lost. I am looking for the house of some friends, where I am to stay the night."

The policeman continued to smile, holding the cigar between his fingers a few inches from his mouth. "Perhaps I can help you. I know everyone here." He put the cigar back into his mouth, squinted and took a deep drag while he waited for Enrique's response.

Enrique knew that if he was going to keep up with Felipe that he would have to act fast. "Oh, *muy bien.* They are two brothers."

The policeman tilted his head slightly. "Two brothers?"

"Si," Enrique said. *"Los hermanos Cajones."*

The two men behind the policeman exchanged glances. The policeman wrinkled his brow. "Cajones?"

"Si," Enrique said, then swiftly kicked the policeman between his legs, from which he

buckled and groaned, and Enrique grabbed him by the front of his shirt and tossed him into the two men causing them to lose their footing and fall backward.

Enrique ran quickly into the street and he had run several meters before he caught up with Felipe. Before the boy could react Enrique had him by the shirt collar and dragged him off the street and into an alley. He pinned the boy against the wall and looked down into his frightened eyes. Felipe tried to kick his shin and get away but Enrique was ready for that.

"You are coming back to the *hacienda* with me," Enrique said. "But first I need you to take me to Amado."

The boy squirmed trying to get away. "No, I do not want to!"

"Listen to me! Your family is very worried. There are people who love you that miss you."

"I do not care about them!"

"Felipe, do you think Sosa really cares about you?"

Felipe did not seem prepared for such a question and looked up at Enrique with confusion. "He loves us. He tells us that he does."

"That is a lie. All Sosa cares about is money and power. And he will use you to get it, even if it gets you killed. Including Amado, and Javier. And he will not shed a single tear."

"No! You are a liar!" Felipe tried to get away again, and sudden noises from the street caused them both to turn and look. It was the policeman barking orders at his two men. Felipe screamed to get their attention, and it worked, and they all started running toward Enrique.

Enrique grabbed Felipe by the wrist and started running. The boy tried but couldn't fight off Enrique's strong hold and eventually ran with him. Enrique turned a corner sharply and after running only a few meters, he noticed a dark, narrow space between two buildings and dragged Felipe into it. Once well hidden he backed up against a wall and pulled Felipe to him, placing a hand over the boy's mouth muffling his screams.

Only a few seconds passed before the policeman and his two men ran by, and rather than go back out into the street, Enrique went the opposite direction and followed the narrow space all the way to another street, and when he felt it was safe, he dragged the boy into the open and all the way to the livery.

The livery attendant came walking in

holding a lit lantern head high, and when he noticed Enrique and the boy, he stopped and stared.

Enrique nodded his chin toward the horse and buggy that he had parked in the stable. "*Señor,* I need you to remove the horse from the harness. I will need to borrow a bridle and saddle. You can hold my buggy as security until I return them to you."

The attendant stepped a little closer and held the lantern a little higher. He was an old man, hair very gray and skin swarthy and wrinkled, wearing white cotton, a brown woven vest, and sandals on his dusty feet. He looked under sagging eyelids at the boy, then back at Enrique. "I have lived in Hermosillo all of my life. I have lived those years quietly and minded my own business. But I am sick of what Sosa has done to this city and its people. Many of them are too afraid to confront him, or too influenced by the money. I am happy to help you."

"Gracias, señor," Enrique said, then turned the boy and looked directly at him. "I need you to tell me where I can find Amado."

Felipe said nothing, and only looked at Enrique with frightened eyes that welled with tears, and he blinked them in dual streams down his cheek.

Enrique got down on his knees and held

on to the boy's arms more compassionately and less forceful. "You heard what the man said, and you heard what I have said. Now I need you to think about how much you care about your brother, and tell me where I can find him."

Felipe looked down at his feet for a few seconds, then back up at Enrique. "Are you one of *El Trio*?"

Enrique thought for a moment, and realized the boy needed to believe in someone. "Yes, that is the name they are calling us."

"I hear you are good with a bow and arrow. Will you teach me?"

A warm feeling came over Enrique, and he smiled and nodded. "It would be my pleasure, Felipe."

The boy wiped at his tears. "Then I will take you to Amado."

After the incident in the cotton field, Pang had spent most of the day following Fernando, and was not surprised when the field supervisor went straight to him after Pang had intervened with the field worker. The Chinaman was very good at moving from place to place without being noticed, or when someone came by, he put on his tourist act, which was no more than walking with his hands behind his back, whistling, observing his surroundings, and offering a friendly nod to anyone he met. The people of the *hacienda* were comfortable with him now, so he was able to pull it off very well.

Now that it was dark, it was easier to be more prudent, but more so to hide, which he did in a stall inside the stable, once he had followed Fernando there. He was alarmed to find Jorge, the supervisor from the cotton field, holding the stable worker by the neck and pinned up against the wall. Fernando approached them slowly and methodically, looking straight into the eyes of the terrified stable worker.

Jorge grinned at Fernando. "He has something he wants to tell you."

Fernando nodded. "Okay, let go of him."

The stable worker coughed a bit, then held his throat. He glanced fearfully at Jorge.

"Go ahead," Jorge said. "Tell him."

"The man Enrique — of *El Trio* — he left here in a horse and buggy, dressed as a businessman."

Fernando took one step closer. "Where was he going?"

"I don't know exactly — but to look for the boy, Amado."

Fernando nodded and looked at Jorge. "You better ride into town and warn Sosa. And quickly. It's hard to tell what that *Cri-*

ollo is up to."

As Jorge turned to leave, Pang walked out of the stall and into the opening stopping Jorge in his tracks. He was surprised at first, but eventually he smiled. "Well, it's *el Chino.*"

Fernando turned to acknowledge him as well, but said nothing.

Pang bowed slightly. "Good evening, gentlemen."

"What do you want?" Fernando said.

"I was just out for an evening walk, and I ran into you fine gentlemen." Pang pointed a hand toward the stable attendant. "I was hoping to have a word with him, about my horse, but I will wait until you are done."

Jorge took two steps closer to Pang, his eyes glaring. "Maybe you and I should have a talk . . . since now your knee is not in my back."

"Well, that is fine, but I would rather talk to the stableman first. Then I can talk to you. Business before pleasure, you know."

"You'll find no pleasure in me beating your ass to a bloody pulp."

"I can see that your mood is not good. Perhaps I should come back another time."

After Pang turned to walk away he closed his eyes, and focused intently on the sounds around him. He heard the motion and the footsteps, and like a dragonfly hovering over a stream, he darted sideways, causing Jorge to lose his balance and fall into the dusty floor of the stable.

Pang took his proper fighting stance, feet spread apart, knees slightly bent, hands elongated in front of his chest.

Jorge jumped back on his feet, eyes wide inside a dusty face. After three deep, panting breaths he growled and charged Pang, who merely shifted his weight to one foot and extended the other leg to an angle, once again tripping Jorge to a sliding, dusty landing on the barn floor.

Jorge was not as quick to jump to his feet this time, but he was fuming mad. His third charge was much slower and calculated, but it ended with a blunt kick to the knee, then a sharp jab to the jaw. He fell to the floor with a belching groan, and then wiped at the blood that trickled from inside his mouth and down over his lips. Though slow to rise to his feet, he kept a glaring stare on Pang, and was about to engage when a stern voice stopped him.

"Enough!" Fernando said, walking toward them. Jorge, breathing hard, shifted his glance back and forth between the two men. Pang kept his eyes focused on Jorge.

Fernando stepped to where Pang could

see him. "What do you want?"

Pang relaxed his stance. "We will all go now to see Señora Ramírez."

Fernando narrowed his eyes. "Why?"

"Or I can save you the embarrassment of getting fired. You can just leave." Pang nodded toward Jorge. "And take this imbecile with you."

Fernando grunted and smiled. "She will not believe anything you say."

"I am prepared to take that chance. I have watched you all day. I know how you treat her people. There are many witnesses. Yes, they are scared of you, but all they need is a friend to stand up for them. Yes . . . if not today, tomorrow, or the next day, neither of you will be employed at this *hacienda.* I will make sure of it."

Jorge brushed the dust off of his hands and spat onto the floor. "I say we just kill this *Chino* and be done with all of it."

Pang nodded. "You are welcome to try."

Jorge took deep, rapid breaths, as Fernando glared at the Chinaman.

"Well," Pang said. "What will it be?"

Fernando's eyes darted around nervously. "You cannot beat Sosa."

"And that is why you side with him? Or is it because you are evil like him?"

"You don't understand. If Sosa wants you

on his side, he either gets what he wants, or he kills you. Everyone would be better off just letting him have his way."

Pang spoke through pinched lips. "You are a coward."

Jorge shouted. "Let's kill him!"

Fernando turned to him angrily. "Silence!" Jorge seemed more humiliated from his *jefe*'s response than after he'd crawled up from the barn floor.

Pang looked Fernando directly and sternly into his eyes. "Don't let Sosa's spell of fear overcome you. Choose now, and you will have us on your side. United as people we can defeat him. But not without courage."

Fernando glanced at both men while he pondered Pang's plea. "Turning my back on Sosa will be a certain death sentence."

"You don't think your life is not already at great risk? Sosa will use you only to benefit him. His will is not for the people. And your life means nothing to him. Show your loyalty to Constanza Ramírez and then you will have the same loyalty returned to you."

Fernando once again looked at Jorge. At that moment Sereno walked inside the stable and stopped and stood near the main double doors. They all acknowledged him with a passing glance, and then Fernando returned his attention to Pang. "We have another problem. Many of my field hands, and Jorge is one of them, are paid by Sosa to look the other way. What do we do about them?"

Pang looked at Jorge, who glared at each of them angrily, but the Chinaman was not worried about Jorge, or people like him. "Can you make a list of these people?"

Fernando nodded. *"Si, puedo."*

"Good. We will meet with Señora Ramírez, and you will show her this list. My suggestion to her will be that we find out where the hearts of the people truly are, and give them the chance to decide whose side they are really on."

Jorge spat on the ground. "I will never go back to being a laborer. I would rather die! *Viva* Sosa!" He ran past the men and through the doors into the night.

Pang nodded at Sereno. "You better go warn Enrique. This is about to get very ugly."

In the blackness of night Enrique and Felipe rode double down the dirt street, heading toward the cobblestone thoroughfare that led them to the headquarters where Amado was said to be. Save a few dim lanterns, there was very little light, and other than an occasional howl from a cantina, Hermosillo was a city at rest.

Enrique did not care much for this name, *El Trio,* but after seeing the look in Felipe's eyes, he realized how important the legend was, that everyone, not just boys, needed something to believe in. It reminded him of his days growing up at the Tumacácori mission, and the hope that Father Gaeta gave him. In the beginning it wasn't so much the teachings of God, or the education in general, but the promise to help him become a better, stronger man. To get justice, that was what Enrique knew he needed, and that was what he got. Felipe was no different, and neither was any other boy, Enrique thought. It was just a matter of finding a way to reach them.

As they turned down the cobblestone street the horse's footsteps echoed in the quiet of the city, stirring only a man passed out drunk against the wall of an adobe. A sudden noise forced Enrique to stop his horse so the footsteps didn't drown out the noise.

"What is it?" Felipe said, leaning around Enrique's back to look into the night.

Enrique heard the noise again, which caused him to smile and look toward an alley ahead. "Felipe, *mi amigo,* it is time you met Sereno."

Enrique dismounted in the alley, leaving Felipe on the horse, and he led the animal by the reins until he eventually saw Sereno appear out of the darkness. Sereno told him in sign language what had happened with Pang and Fernando, and it was enough for Enrique to know that Sosa was not going to be happy, and that they would have to help Constanza Ramírez form a defense. He instructed Sereno to go back and help Pang keep an eye on things, then returned to the saddle.

"What are we going to do?" Felipe said.

"We have to find Amado, and quickly."

Enrique spurred the horse down the dark alley, and the shod hooves caused a discordant racket on the cobblestone street. Though he feared the noise might disturb many people from their sleep, and he did not like to attract this kind of attention, he figured that they might as well be prepared for the ensuing storm, because at this point protecting Amado was too important.

Enrique was not surprised that Felipe led him back to the same adobe headquarters where he was once imprisoned. It was Colonel Rodríguez who was assigned to give Amado soldier training. Discipline, saluting, marching, physical training, training in firearms, explosives — all things that make a young, impressionable boy's eyes wide and heart beat with excitement. It would all end with a special patch sewed on to his khaki uniform, which advanced him from the level of courier to fighting soldier. Felipe mentioned how Amado would point out this patch on another soldier's chest and how they all looked on with admiration. Enrique knew it was the bait that lured these youngsters into Sosa's snare. To draw them away meant more than finding different bait, but ridding their mind of the ideology that Sosa and his men preached, and a reward much greater than martyrdom.

They were a city block away when Enrique stopped the horse and dismounted, and helped Felipe down. They led the horse by the reins and tied it to a nearby hitching post, then walked quietly to where the building was in view. The lanterns on the front entrance lit the area enough that they could see the two guards.

Enrique whispered. "We will have to find a different, quiet way in."

Felipe tapped him on the shoulder, then motioned with his index finger for Enrique to follow. The boy crept through the alley and to another street that led to the side of the headquarters. When they got to the dark side of the building Felipe led them through the darkness to a telegraph pole that was only inches from the adobe wall. Before Enrique could say anything the boy was wrapping his arms and legs around the pole and working his way up. He was impressed to see that Felipe was experienced enough with pole climbing that he made fists to avoid splinters, and relied mostly on his inner thighs and arms to do the climbing. Though not nearly as limber, and especially in a dress suit, Enrique removed his hat and flung in into the alley, then did his best to follow along. Within a minute's time they both found themselves on top of the building. They crawled slowly across the low pitch, careful not to slip on the red clay tiles that lined the entire roof. Felipe cleverly worked his way to the ridge which proved to be much safer and easier to pace on their hands and knees. The boy stopped at an opening that led down into a courtyard, which Enrique had never seen before, but agreed that this was a good way to enter with the limited risk of attracting attention of the guards. The courtyard was lit with a lantern at each corner, and Felipe pointed at a guard who sat on a chair, and had fallen asleep.

They moved to an area over a garden trellis covered in a grapevine, which Felipe was quick to lower himself onto and climb down into the courtyard. Enrique waited until the boy was on the ground to attempt the climb himself, and when Felipe looked up at him and nodded, he swung his foot over the edge of the roof. Doing so, his foot slipped on a loose tile which sent the clay piece stumbling down and crashing on the stone floor below. Felipe quickly hid behind the trellis and Enrique swung his leg back up and hunkered down out of view. The crashing tile startled the guard from his sleep, and he jumped from the chair with rifle in hand and looked all around to see where the noise came from. Enrique was surprised to see that the guard just stood there and did not walk around and inspect the area, but rather, he shrugged it off and went back to his chair, and within a minute, his chin was against his chest and he was back to his slumber.

Enrique peeked back over the edge and Felipe had come back out from behind the trellis and motioned for him to come down. Before attempting it again, Enrique ran his hand gently along the edge of the roof inspecting for more loose tiles. They seemed secure enough that he went ahead and swung his leg wider over the edge and reached both a hand and foot down to grab a hold of the trellis. He didn't make ground as quick as Felipe, but eventually he was there and, to his amazement, without waking the guard.

They snuck around the opposite side of the courtyard to a hallway that led to the back of the building. This area was away from the jail cells and officer's quarters, which were the only parts Enrique was familiar with. When they came up to a doorway Felipe signaled with the push of his hand for Enrique to back up against the wall and stay there. Felipe, Enrique realized, was in his uniform and not considered a threat, so the sight of him certainly wouldn't be alarming. The boy entered the doorway and Enrique peeked around to see that it was a sleeping barracks for the soldiers in training. There were no guards anywhere to be seen, but waking any of the sleeping men would be dangerous for Enrique, not as much for Felipe.

When Felipe found the bunk of Amado, he woke him and encouraged him to get up and follow him. Enrique backed away from the door and when the boys came jogging through, the surprise in Amado's eyes, when he saw Enrique standing there, was like a trigger to an alarm. But with a gentle tug of Amado's arm, Felipe kept him quiet and lured him out of the building into the back alley.

Amado couldn't take his eyes off of Enrique, and he looked as though he could erupt with anger at any moment.

"Amado," Felipe whispered, "this is Enrique. A man of *El Trio*! He is famous!"

Amado glared at Felipe. "He is the enemy!"

Felipe grabbed both of Amado's arms and pleaded with him. "No, he is our friend, and he will teach us many great things about how to help our people. Sosa will not do these things. He will only send you to your death."

"What is so bad about dying?" Amado said. "I would rather die a hero than work for a worthless peso."

Enrique squatted and looked up into Amado's eyes with the hope that a new eye level would not be as intimidating. "Amado, there is nothing in this world more valuable than family. You have a family, at home waiting for you. Sosa is not your family. He is a businessman using people for his own gain. You need to realize this."

Amado grimaced and spat at Enrique's feet. "You know nothing, *Criollo*! I will never salute you!"

"That is just it, Amado. I will never ask

you to salute anyone. This is your chance to be your own man, be free, and live for yourself. If Sosa wins, and he has his way, no one will ever be free. They will only do what is good for him and no one else. No one will have anything unless he approves of it."

Amado looked angrily at Felipe. "How can you believe anything this man says? If you go back with him to the *hacienda,* you will become a traitor and die!"

"No, Amado," Enrique said, "that is not true."

"It is true!" Amado said. "Sosa is going to take over the *hacienda,* and everyone there will either work for him or die. It is his commandment!"

"Sosa would like you to believe that he is God, but he is just a man, like any other man, only with evil in his heart, and who will kill the only people in the world who love you if you don't help us stop him."

Felipe stepped directly in front of Amado, a look of excitement on his face. "Amado, Enrique will show us how to shoot his bow and arrows! It is the weapon he used to bring down the Demon Warrior and his bandits. It has magical powers!"

Enrique was quite taken by the boy's imagination, but at the same time it was a perfect example of just how impressionable he was, and how horrible it was for any man to be putting such a young soul at risk.

Amado, however, a couple years older, was not so easy to persuade. He looked at Enrique with a deep contempt. It was possible, Enrique thought, that Amado was in too deep. To ask him about the whereabouts of his grandfather could possibly be a step in the wrong direction. Sure, there was a great risk of time and waiting too long, but he knew he had to win the lad's heart first, and then he will help.

"No," Amado said, pushing Felipe away and continuing to glare at Enrique. "Because Felipe is my brother, I will forgive this moment ever happened. But next time I will not forgive. I will only fight, and kill to the death."

Felipe drew a deep, mournful stare. "Amado?"

Enrique stood up straight and put a hand on Felipe's shoulder. "Come on, Felipe."

"Amado," Felipe cried. *"Por favor?"*

Amado did not answer.

Enrique nudged the boy away and before they could make another step Amado was gone, out of the alley, out of sight, and Enrique feared that neither he nor his brother would ever see him alive again.

CHAPTER SEVEN

The night was fading fast and the haze of early dawn was at their backs as their horse loped into the courtyard. Rather than go to the stable they went directly to the home of Emanuela, a small two-room adobe built especially as a residence for the teacher of the *hacienda.* She answered the door with sleepy eyes, a woven shawl draped around her shoulders, and she clutched it tightly in the front. Her eyes opened much wider when she saw Felipe.

The boy ran inside to her and they embraced. When she looked up at Enrique her eyes were now welled with tears. *"Gracias."*

Enrique only smiled. "It is better that he not go outside for a while. Sosa and his men will be looking for him."

"I will find a safe place for him," Emanuela said.

"I must be going," Enrique said.

Emanuela stood and stepped toward

Enrique. "Amado?"
Enrique shook his head.
Emanuela looked away in fear.
Enrique put his hand gently on the side of her face. "Pray for him. For now that is all that you can do."
Emanuela looked softly into his eyes, and then suddenly a solemn demeanor came about her. "Fernando and Jose came here only moments ago. All of the field workers and members of the *hacienda* are to meet in the courtyard first thing this morning. Constanza will be addressing them."
Enrique could tell that there was something serious going on, but also that this was a bittersweet moment for Emanuela. He was sure she was happy to have Felipe back, but keeping him safe would be an ongoing duty. And there was still Amado to worry about. "Then I will see you there."

Shortly after Enrique arrived at his room, and he freshened up and changed back into his regular clothes, a knock came from his door. It was Pang, and after a briefing on what happened with Fernando and Jorge, Pang and Enrique walked down to meet Fernando, and all three went to the dining room to meet with Constanza.
Her face turned ashen, and she was vis-

ibly astonished and shaken when Fernando confessed to his involvement with Sosa. She stood from her chair and walked closer to him, looking deep into his fearful eyes, and then pointed toward the door. "Leave now. And don't ever come back to this *hacienda* again, or I will have you shot on sight."

Enrique and Pang exchanged glances.

Fernando put his hands in a praying position and shook them in front of his chest. "Please, *señora,* I beg you to not make me leave. I will do whatever you say to prove my loyalty to you."

Constanza only looked at him with disgust and spoke through tightened lips. "How can you stand here and say that, after Sosa murdered my husband and son, to me the most precious human beings in the world!"

"I know, *señora*! Please understand I was very afraid!"

Enrique stepped around the table and motioned for Fernando to rise from his chair. "Fernando, let us talk with Señora Ramírez for a moment. Please wait outside."

After Fernando left the room, Enrique encouraged Constanza to sit down, and he and Pang sat across from each other. Enrique nodded at Pang.

"Señora," Pang said. "I understand how betrayed you must feel, and how impossible

it may be to ever trust Fernando again. But I want you to consider how better it might be to have him here where we can watch him, rather than with Sosa, or out in hiding."

Constanza slammed a fist on the table. "I should have him shot!"

Pang nodded. "That is the reaction of anger. Give your heart and mind time to settle, and then let's make the wisest decision together. One that is best for the *hacienda.*"

Constanza took a deep breath, and then nodded. "All right, but what do we do with him in the meantime?"

Pang looked at Enrique, who obliged them with a response.

"Let him stay on the *hacienda,*" Enrique said, "but relieve him of his duties, and insist he have no interaction with the workers. Sereno and Pang will help keep an eye on him until a better decision can be made. As of now, we have more important matters to discuss."

Enrique nodded at Pang, who produced the paper list of people Fernando identified as working for Sosa. He handed the list to Constanza.

"What is this?" Constanza said, unfolding the paper.

"Fernando prepared it," Pang said. "It is a list of all supervisors and field workers who have succumbed to Sosa's influence."

Constanza read down the list with added astonishment.

Pang held up a hand. "But before we react, I want you to understand that most if not nearly all of these people only did so out of fear, and would truly side with us if they knew they had protection from Sosa."

Constanza dropped the list on the table in front of her and gazed forward in thought. "And I thought it couldn't get any worse."

"Let's look at it in a different way," Enrique said, getting her attention. "Fernando called a meeting of all the supervisors and field workers. In this meeting you can address all of them on what is surely to come with Sosa. Assure them that we have a plan to defeat Sosa, and that we will. Build their confidence in you, and relieve them of their fear."

"How do we do such a thing?" Constanza asked.

Enrique smirked at Pang, then back at Constanza. "We have just the plan for that."

Though the sun was up there was still a chill in the air as scores of field workers, men and women of all ages, and some children, gathered in the courtyard, straw sombreros on their heads, cotton sacks at their sides, some carrying tools, such as hoes or makeshift shovels. The supervisors, who rode horseback, all dismounted and stood nearby, holding the reins. Sereno stood against a building, not far away, peeling an orange and peeking around at the commencement. As promised, Fernando and Jose were there to greet them, and next to them were Constanza, Enrique, and Pang. Eventually Enrique sought out Emanuela in the crowd, standing with Felipe, who now wore regular clothes. Though Emanuela smiled at him, it was a solemn gathering, and such an event that none of them were used to.

Fernando stepped out of the way and let Constanza step forward to address the crowd. She held the list in her hand, as if it were a weapon, and sternly and slowly scanned the crowd studying all of their faces.

"I know many of you live in fear," she said. "Ever since Sosa killed my husband, and my son, you have anxiously awaited the moment when he returns and makes his final call. This meeting is to let you know that if Sosa has made an attempt to bribe you, to lure you away from your loyalty here, that I do not blame you if you accepted his proposal. I understand that it is inconceivable that an old woman can outwit such a powerful man with his own army. For that understanding, I forgive you for your fear, or for your lack of confidence, and at this very moment, before we plant another seed, or prune another tree, we all need to decide our future."

She paused a moment and let them absorb her words.

"I am not sure I would have been able to come up with the will or the faith to defeat Sosa until the men of *El Trio* arrived on our *hacienda.* Through their talents, bravery, and wisdom, I have found both the will and the faith. Now it is only important that you believe in them too. With them, we have made a plan, and with God on our side we will never have to give up this *hacienda* to anyone and it will forever be in our name, and you will all forever be free."

The people of the crowd exchanged glances, and many of them nodded toward Enrique and Pang and whispered comments to one another.

Constanza held the list up in the air. "I do not care what Sosa has promised you, or what you agreed to, but we can forget it all right now." Constanza ripped the paper into pieces, which stirred the crowd to broken moans.

One man in the crowd raised his fist into the air. *"Viva Hacienda de Ramírez! Viva!"*

The rest of the crowd followed progressively. *"Viva! Viva!"*

Felipe stepped forward and raised his fist into the air. *"Viva El Trio! Viva!"*

As before, the crowd followed his chant. *"Viva! Viva!"*

As Constanza expected, nearly all of the field workers stayed on the *hacienda* and pledged their sincere loyalty. Only the family of Jorge, his two brothers, their wives and children, left to join Sosa. When Constanza met with them, she could see it in the brother's eyes. Not just the hatred, but more so the greed, which fueled it all. Regardless of how their women felt, there was nothing she could do or say, she just had to let them go.

To formulate their plan against Sosa, Enrique and Pang met with them in groups, the workers from the cotton fields, from the orange groves, the stable workers, the house servants, the guards, and even Emanuela, the teacher. During each meeting Constanza was present, as was Jose. They talked about the upcoming fiesta, *Día de la Consti-*

tución, on February 5, and how during such events were when Sosa liked to catch people by surprise.

"It may be the day he comes, or it may not," Constanza said, "but we will be prepared for any day."

Enrique met with the guards, and a lieutenant named Victor, who was promoted to head of security, in place of Fernando. They discussed their inventory of weapons and ammunition, and though nothing compared to Sosa's arsenal, Enrique assured them, if used properly, it would be plenty. In separate shifts, the guards would train the people of the *hacienda* how to load and shoot the rifles, as well as in target practice. They were not expected to be expert marksmen, only to become familiar with the weapons and increase their chances of a good defense.

Pang also arranged meetings in the stable with each and every one of the people of the *hacienda,* and taught them all how to use their hands and feet in hand-to-hand combat. He taught them methods of breathing, and exercising the muscles of the body. He assured them that constant practice of these methods would make their bodies a weapon as powerful as a sword.

Fernando was not involved with any of the planning events, and agreed to serve a jail sentence at the *hacienda* for his betrayal. Very few knew about the hidden rooms, under ground and next to the wine cellar, which were well hidden behind hinged racks of wine bottles. Though built for protection, as a hiding place, the doors typically locked from the inside, but locks were also installed on the outside just for such a situation as with Fernando. He was placed in one of the rooms and two guards were assigned to protect the wine cellar. This was the only way that Constanza could be certain that Fernando would not change his mind and return to Sosa, or reveal their plans to him. Two of the other rooms were made known to Emanuela, and that at the first sign of trouble, she was to take Felipe and the other children there to hide. Children, Constanza said, would not be allowed to fight, and they must be protected.

In the room upstairs at the *Cantina de El Manadero,* Guadalupe sat in a chair beside Sosa holding a plate of fruit — red grapes, strawberries, peeled mandarins — and fed them to him one at a time, occasionally putting a strawberry between her teeth and delivering it to him mouth to mouth. They were laughing at one another when a knock came to the door, and Sosa was enjoying himself too much to answer. The knock came again.

"What is it?" Sosa yelled.

"It's Colonel Rodríguez, *patrón. Esta muy importante.*"

Guadalupe shoved a grape in Sosa's mouth, and he talked as he chewed. "What could be more important than this?" They both laughed, and Rodríguez knocked again. "All right, All right!" Sosa yelled. *"Entre — entre."*

Guadalupe stood up and stepped aside as Rodríguez came through the door with Jorge behind him. Jorge nervously removed his sombrero and held it in front of him with both hands.

Sosa acknowledged them both. "Yes, what is it?"

"This is Jorge, from the *Hacienda de Ramírez.* He is one of ours, and is here to report that he has been discovered."

Sosa's face turned grim as he stood from his chair and opened a cigar box on his desk. He retrieved a cigar, cut off the tip, stuck it in his teeth and lit it with a match. He puffed several times, creating thick clouds of smoke around him. He removed the cigar and nodded as he squinted through the haze. "How were you discovered?"

"El Chino," Jorge said. "He confronted us."

"Us?" Sosa said.

"*Si, patrón.* Me and our *jefe,* Fernando Jiménez."

Sosa nodded. "And where is Fernando now?"

Jorge lowered his head slightly. "He did not come."

"What do you mean he did not come?"

Jorge swallowed. "He would not be disloyal to Señora Ramírez."

Sosa pointed his cigar toward the door. "Okay, leave us. I will talk to the colonel about this."

Jorge nodded and left the room. When the door was shut, Sosa addressed his colonel. "What is happening?"

"Apparently Señora Ramírez has hired *El Trio* to defend her *hacienda.* They are seeking out anyone who is disloyal, and firing them."

"So . . . this Jorge, do you trust him?"

"*Si, patrón.* He left by choice, as did his entire family. They are with us now."

Sosa took a healthy drag on the cigar, and then waved it around as he spoke. "His family?"

"*Si,* his wife and children, his two brothers, and their wives and children. They are all in Hermosillo, waiting for your command."

"I see." Sosa walked over to Guadalupe and ran the knuckle of his index finger gently down her cheek.

"What do you want me to do, *patrón*?" Rodríguez said.

"What else do you have for me?"

"We are also missing one of the boys, a courier, Felipe Ortega. Amado says he does not know what happened to his brother. Neither does Javier."

"And you believe them?"

Rodríguez paused, which caused Sosa to turn his head sharply and look at him for an answer.

"Well?" Sosa said.

"No, I do not believe Amado."

"And why is this?"

"One of the soldiers in training witnessed Amado getting up in the middle of the night, and following Felipe outside. He thought nothing of it until Felipe disappeared."

Sosa nodded in thought. "Well then, there is nothing else to do with this matter."

"Patrón?"

Sosa looked sternly at the colonel. "The boy lied. He must be made an example to others. We cannot have this among our youth, correct?"

"Correct, *patrón.*"

"Have the other boy do it."
"Other boy?"
"*Si,* Javier. He is still with us, right?"
"*Si, patrón.* Have him do what?"
"Shoot him, what else?"
Rodríguez looked at Sosa in horror, and glanced at Guadalupe, who also gazed back at him with a similar fear.
"There is no tolerance for lying," Sosa continued. "Death is the only suitable punishment. And having the boy do it . . . it will teach him a hard lesson early, and to harden his heart and be strong." Sosa studied Rodríguez for a moment. "Am I clear on that . . . *coronel*?"
Rodríguez responded without hesitation. *"Si, patrón."*
After responding Rodríguez turned and headed for the door, and as he reached for the doorknob, Sosa interrupted his departure.
"Oh, and colonel?"
Rodríguez turned to face Sosa.
Sosa held his smoldering cigar near his mouth as he spoke. "This Jorge . . . and his brothers."
"Si, patrón?"
"Shoot them too."
Rodríguez paused for only a second. "But why, *patrón*? They were loyal to you."

"But they were not supposed to get caught. We needed them there, not here. They are of no use to us now, and we will have to make a new strategy for the *hacienda.*" Sosa once again looked at Guadalupe, but kept talking to Rodríguez. "And colonel, after you kill the men, bring the women to Guadalupe." He smiled at her. "Since they are good at bearing children, I am sure she will find a use for their skills."

Without hesitation, Colonel Rodríguez saluted Sosa.

"And colonel," Sosa said. "Send in Chavón. That is all for now."

"Si, patrón."

After Rodríguez left the room, Sosa sat back down in his chair and looked up in thought puffing on his cigar.

Guadalupe walked over to him, leaned over and kissed him on the forehead. "I am going now, *mi amor.*"

"Where are you going?"

"I have business to tend to. And you just gave me more work to do."

Sosa nodded and watched her walk to the door, and when she opened it, Chavón was on the other side. She told him to go in, and he walked around her toward the desk and she left the room.

Chavón nodded at Sosa. "You asked for me?"

"*Si.* Fernando Jiménez, our man at the *hacienda* . . . he has betrayed us, and pledged his loyalty to Constanza Ramírez. I need you to plan a way into the *hacienda,* find him, and rid the world of his presence."

Chavón smirked. "*Si, patrón.* My pleasure."

"And now, we have no other choice but to make our move on the *hacienda.* Even though we do not have our informants, they will stand no chance against our armed men. Let's go ahead with our plans as usual, but only sooner."

"When, *patrón*? We still have not received the new shipment of weapons."

"Have they reached the port at Bahía?"

"We have not received word, yet. The smugglers are bypassing the port and bringing them through the estuary."

"Send a party of men now. Have them meet with Vázquez and track them until they find them. I want the weapons back here as soon as possible."

"*Si, patrón.* Once they are back, I will get our men ready for the attack. What day shall we prepare for?"

Sosa smiled after a long exhale of smoke. "There is only one day . . . and it will be a fiesta for everyone."

Guadalupe left the through the back door without being noticed, and walked down the alley, and continued through the back alleys hoping she wouldn't be seen. When she reached the stable she asked for a horse, a sombrero, and a poncho. The stable worker asked no questions and gave her what she asked. After she put on the hat and poncho, the stable worker opened the doors, and she mounted the horse and dashed through the opening, gouging her heels into the animal forcing it to a gallop.

She raced through town, weaving through pedestrians, *policía,* cutting off other riders and buggies, attracting a lot of attention, but no one knew it was Guadalupe Rojas. It took her ten minutes to reach the *Hacienda de Ramírez,* and her galloping horse grabbed the attention of the field workers, and ultimately the armed guards, who lowered their guns in preparation for a possible intrusion. But she stopped abruptly in the courtyard and pushed the sombrero backward until it fell and was caught by the chin cord.

When the guards noticed it was a woman, they were more at ease, but one of the guards had already summoned Constanza

Ramírez. In a matter of a few seconds, Constanza was outside the front door with Jose, Enrique, and Pang, all at full attention and tailing close by.

"What is this all about?" Constanza said, looking curiously at the woman.

Guadalupe dismounted and led the horse closer.

When Constanza had a better look at her face, she scowled. "What is this whore doing on my *hacienda*?"

"Por favor, señora," Guadalupe said, her face wrought with fear. "I have something very important to tell you."

Constanza looked on with disgust. "What would Sosa's whore have to tell me that would ever interest me?"

Enrique tugged gently on Constanza's arm. "*Señora,* why don't we hear what she has to say?"

"It could be one of Sosa's tricks!"

"Possibly," Enrique said, "but it is just her, and neither of us will let anything happen to you."

Constanza took a deep breath as she studied Guadalupe's solemn gaze. "All right, what is it?"

Guadalupe took two steps closer. "It is Amado. Sosa . . . he is going to kill him, and I cannot stand for it."

Enrique's face now grew long with great concern. "How do you know this?"

"I heard him myself . . . give the orders to Colonel Rodríguez. Felipe abandoned Sosa, and Amado lied about it . . . to protect his brother."

Enrique looked at Constanza. "We must do something."

"There is something else," Guadalupe said.

"What?" Enrique said.

"It is awful. Javier . . . he is the one who will kill Amado."

They all looked on in shock.

"Por favor," Guadalupe said, with tears in her eyes. "Sosa . . . he is a monster! I knew of nowhere else to go!"

Enrique nodded. "You did the right thing." He looked at Constanza. "I believe her. And I am going to stop this."

Amado was stripped of his uniform, now wearing nothing but a white pima shirt that barely covered his genitals. He was tied to a tall pole, with hemp rope around his wrists high above his head and his feet barely touching the ground. The pole was already stained with the blood of other men, accused of whatever injustice Sosa thought them to be guilty of. It was planted in dusty ground, not far from an adobe wall riddled with bullet holes, and in an open area in the busiest part of Hermosillo, where the presence of a few *policía* and two horses pulling a prisoner wagon were sure to bring on many spectators. The crowds of spectators now, however, were not just civilians, but also the youth in training, the soldiers from the barracks, ordered to be there, because this was the most valuable lesson they could ever learn: never defy Sosa.

Colonel Rodríguez had led the party in on horseback, and now he walked into the open area, dragging Javier by the arm, regardless of the boy's doleful pleas.

"No, *por favor,* I can't do it!"

Javier fell to his knees, less than four yards from battered and bloody Amado. Colonel Rodríguez lifted him up by the shirt collar. "On your feet!" Once the boy was sturdy, the colonel shoved a rifle into his hands. "You want to learn how to be a man? Learn to harden your heart against the enemy, or they will defeat you!"

Javier's hands shook and his jaw quivered as he looked at his friend, Amado, hanging there, weak and powerless. He gazed around at the crowd, at the many spectators, the guards, and the other prisoners in the steel caged wagon, and was horrified at how they all looked at him with expectation.

The colonel forced the gun upward, and pushed the butt against the boy's shoulder. "Aim like you were trained to do!"

Javier squinted down through the sights and across the barrel and blinked the tears out of his eyes. Eventually the blurry image of his friend became clearer, and he was overwhelmed with emotion. He closed his eyes, lowered his head away from the rifle, and wept.

Colonel Rodríguez grabbed the rifle from his hands with one hand, and Javier's neck with the other. He looked down into the tearful boy's eyes. "You either do your duty, or I will tie you to that pole and shoot you both!"

Javier took several deep breaths and the colonel handed the gun back to him. The boy accepted it with much apprehension, but he put the stock to his shoulder and the colonel stepped back, stood erect and ordered all of his men to attention.

"Ready!" the colonel shouted.

Javier took a firm hold of the rifle, and his finger over the trigger, batting his eyelids for a clearer focus.

The colonel's voice echoed again through the open area. "Aim!"

Amidst the colonel's fading call came a

whiffle, then a thud, and as the colonel groaned, Javier lowered the rifle and looked to find the colonel dropping to his knees with an arrow stuck in his chest. Suddenly through the silence there were screams from the crowd, another arrow claimed one of the guards, and when Javier looked up, the next thing he saw was Enrique running into the open area on horseback. Before he could take another breath, Enrique was upon him, bringing the horse to a sliding halt and creating a dust cloud around them.

Enrique leaned over and extended his hand toward Javier. "Quick, get on!"

Javier grabbed his hand and forearm and he was lifted up behind Enrique. The boy turned his head quickly to the left and peered through the dust at Sereno, also on horseback, who jumped down and cut Amado loose from the pole.

Gunfire quickly erupted, and bullets whizzed all around them. Amado was now on the horse behind Sereno, and they both leaned forward and raced through the open area toward a side street.

Enrique stopped long enough to nock another arrow and sent it sailing into one of the *policía* near the prisoner wagon. Pang was now upon the guards there, and he had dismounted from his horse and was engaged in hand combat, kicking their rifles away, and knocking them unconscious.

Just as Enrique was about to nock another arrow, guards started to drop, one by one, but not from Pang's fighting methods, but from bullets from a gun. After scanning the open area, Enrique looked up and finally found the shooter. It was a gringo on top of the adobe wall, lying on his stomach, his arms resting on their elbows, flipping the lever of the Winchester rifle in perfect unison with his rapid firing.

Before Enrique could make any further acknowledgment, a powerful burn consumed his left shoulder. He leaned forward and put a hand over the burn, and when he removed the hand it was covered with blood. At this point there was nothing more to do than spur his horse and flee the open area. Maybe their guardian angel would show his face later.

Pang suddenly realized that someone was doing his job for him — the guards dropped one by one from gunshots. He found the source — a white man on the adobe wall, firing with precision, and in less than fifteen seconds, the guards lay either dead or out cold. But who was this man?

The man stood up from the adobe wall and jumped back down on the other side.

Pang looked for his friends, then at the pole, and realized their deed was done.

One of the prisoners in the wagon spoke out to him. "Let me out and I will help you."

Pang looked in at him, and at his brothers. "No, Jorge. You had your chance."

The Chinaman quickly found his horse in the crowd, mounted, and in a pluming rush, followed Enrique's trail of dust through the opening and out into the city.

Chapter Eight

Sereno led the way, his horse galloping through the dusty streets, down the cobblestone thoroughfare, and into the countryside toward the *hacienda.* Enrique felt dizzy from his wound, but he leaned forward, keeping his eyes on Sereno, and held on to the reins, with the boy clinging tightly behind him. Occasionally Enrique would peer back, hoping to see that Pang had made it through. Before long, that was exactly what he saw, but not just Pang, there was also that gringo close to the Chinaman's tail. Since the man helped them there was certainly no fear of who he might be, but there was definitely a rising curiosity.

After they all reached the courtyard in front of the main house at the *hacienda,* they were greeted by Constanza, Jose, and Guadalupe, and Emanuela came running from the school yard.

Emanuela was quick to help Amado down

from Sereno's horse. She embraced him with joyful cries and kissed his forehead. She then ran to Javier, who jumped down from Enrique's horse and quickly to her embrace.

Enrique, weak from blood loss, closed his eyes and leaned forward in his saddle.

Emanuela looked at him with concern, and when she saw the blood she called out to the guards. "He is hurt! Please help him down!"

Constanza came running, as did Jose, and after the guards had helped him off the horse Constanza shouted her orders. "Take him to his room, and get our doctor . . . quickly!" Constanza turned to Emanuela, who held both boys close to her. "Emanuela, you take the boys to your place and care for them."

Emanuela nodded, but looked on with great concern for Enrique.

By then time Pang and Sereno had both dismounted they were taking Enrique into the house, but Sereno turned his attention to the man who had ridden in behind Pang, and was now dismounting near a hitching rail. As the man walked closer, his face became clearer under the shadow of a hat brim, and he smiled at them.

Pang followed Sereno's gaze and shaded

his own eyes with his hand. "Sheriff?"

Dutton nodded at Sereno, then reached for Pang's hand and smirked. "I ain't no damned sheriff anymore."

Pang smiled and grabbed Dutton's hand with both of his and held it firmly. "You got my telegram!"

"Beats the Pony Express any day."

Pang's face drew solemn and he pointed behind him. "Enrique, he has been hurt."

The three of them jogged quickly toward the guards as they carried Enrique. The *Criollo* had put each one of his arms around their necks and hobbled along as they carried him into the main house. Everyone followed them, down the halls through the main *casa* and to Enrique's room, where they lay him in his bed.

"Get his shirt off of him," Constanza said to Guadalupe. She turned to Jose and the guards. "Get some hot water and some clean towels." She clapped her hands together. *"Rápidamente!"*

As Guadalupe removed Enrique's bloody shirt, Dutton came forward and stood over him.

Enrique's eyes were half-closed, but he found a slight smile. "Sheriff?" he said in a weedy voice.

Dutton grabbed one of Enrique's hands

and squeezed it firmly. "I'm gonna have to remind you boys about my retirement."

Enrique laughed but it quickly subsided after he winced with pain.

Dutton tapped Enrique's arm gently. "You rest, pardner. I'll let the doctor do his handy work."

Pang led Dutton into the hallway and introduced him to Constanza.

"*Señora,* this is our good friend, Chas Dutton."

Dutton removed his hat and bowed slightly. "My pleasure, ma'am."

"It is nice to meet you, Señor Dutton," Constanza said. "What brings you to Hermosillo?"

"Well —"

Pang interrupted him. "He is here at my request. He is one of *El Trio.*"

"Oh?" Constanza said. "But there are already three of you here."

Dutton's brow wrinkled. "What the hell is *El Trio*?"

Pang put a hand on his shoulder, leaned closer to his ear and whispered. "I will explain later." The Chinaman smiled at Constanza. "*Señora,* it is Mr. Dutton who helped us free Amado and Javier. He is very good with firearms."

Constanza's eyes grew wide with astonishment. "Then it is a blessing you are here, Señor Dutton. Please, let us provide you with a room, and join us for dinner tonight."

"I'm much obliged, ma'am."

Sosa looked down from his horse at the corpse of Colonel Rodríguez, decorated by a protruding arrow in his chest and a blood-soaked shirt. He shifted his gaze to the pole and cut ropes that lay near the base, and then at his dead *policía* that lay all around the prisoner wagon.

Chavón bent over and gripped the arrow tightly, then jerked it out and studied it closely. Blood dripped off of the tip of the primitive arrow. His brow wrinkled as he glanced up at Sosa. "Indian?"

Sosa kept looking around at the scene, his face flush with anger. "That is from no damn Indian." He stopped his gaze at the prisoner wagon, and at Jorge, who peered out at him with a look of desired vengeance. "Go get him."

Chavón looked toward the wagon. "Jorge?"

"*Si,* bring him to me."

Chavón ordered two men to do as Sosa said, and they brought Jorge back, iron fetters around his ankles and wrists. He looked up at Sosa with the same stare.

"You saw everything?" Sosa asked.

Jorge nodded.

"It was *El Trio,* no?"

"*Si,* it was them. And a gringo."

"A gringo?"

"I have never seen him before."

"Very well." Sosa nodded to the guards. "Take him back to the wagon."

Jorge tried to avoid the guards' hold on him. "Wait!"

Sosa looked down at him with surprise.

"The *Criollo,*" Jorge said, "that shot that arrow into the colonel . . . he was wounded. One of the guards shot him."

"Bien," Sosa said, a slight smirk on his face. "Then maybe he will die and my job will be much easier."

"I know where he is staying . . . at the *hacienda.* I can go in there tonight, to the exact room, and I will make sure he is dead. Him and his *Chino* friend."

Sosa pondered his request. "Why do you think I need your help?"

"You don't, *señor.* But I owe it to you."

Sosa glanced at Chavón, who raised his eyebrows and shrugged.

Jorge continued. "Me and my two brothers, we can do it together. We know the place very well, and we know where they are hiding Fernando."

Sosa and Chavón now shared a more serious glance.

Sosa spoke directly at Chavón. "What do you think?"

Chavón nodded. "We could take him with us. It would make it easier to have someone who knew the place."

Sosa studied Jorge's sincerity. "All right, but only on one condition. Your women, and children, they stay with me until the job is done successfully. If you do not succeed, then you will never see them again."

Jorge glanced back and forth between Sosa and Chavón, a bit more nervous than before. "*Si,* I will do it."

Emanuela cleaned Amado's cuts and scrapes around his wrists and ankles, and then prepared a bath for him in a tub outside the back of her *casa.* A privacy curtain, made of woven blankets and hung by a rope that was stretched horizontally across the yard, was pulled around him while he bathed. She took Javier to his mother's, who was drawn to sobs at the sight of him. His mother made him change out of his uniform, and threw the soiled khaki garments into the hearth and they all watched them burn. It was a celebration of sorts, and Emanuela hugged Javier and his mother, kissed them both on the cheeks, and then spoke of the different spell of danger that all of the boys were now under. They each agreed that if and when a new threat ever arose, that they would seek out each other and *El Trio* for protection.

How wonderful it felt to have them back, and safe, Emanuela thought, but her mood was bittersweet in that she could not stop thinking about Enrique. To see such a known hero, weak and in need of help, was heartbreaking. But she laughed at herself when she realized that it was much more than that. She was falling for him.

When she arrived back at her house she checked on Amado, who was now out of the bath and dressed in his normal clothes.

She ran her fingers through his wet hair and smiled at him. "Are you all right, *hermanito*?"

The boy only nodded, and she sensed a great sadness within him.

"Tell me how you are feeling," Emanuela asked.

Amado shrugged. "Felipe was right. And I feel like a fool."

"It takes a man to admit when he is wrong. A real man."

Amado looked into her eyes and she sensed his need for acceptance and understanding.

"I want to do what Felipe wanted," Amado said. "I want to help *El Trio* now."

Emanuela drew a great concern and lowered to her knees and looked dolefully into his eyes. "Amado, there are many things we can do to help *El Trio,* and one of them is to stay out of their way and let them do what they do best."

Amado's eyes brightened. "You should have seen Enrique! He was so fast . . . he shot the arrow from horseback, and killed Colonel Rodríguez before anyone knew what happened. I saw it all with my own eyes and couldn't believe it. No one would want to be like Sosa when they could be like that. Felipe said that Enrique would show him how to shoot the bow and arrow. I want to learn that, too. I want to join *El Trio.*"

"Amado, you can do what you want with your life, but you are still very young. Now that you are here, safe with your family, there will be plenty of time for you to decide what you want."

"But I know things. I know what Sosa is planning. All of these things would be good for *El Trio* to know."

Emanuela let out a long breath, leaned forward, closed her eyes, and laid her head against Amado's chest and hugged him. At that moment she heard running footsteps, leaned back and turned around to find Felipe standing in the opening of the back door, smiling at the sight of Amado. Nothing was said between the two brothers, their sharing of smiles was enough. She also knew that there was nothing she could do to cage these spirited birds, nor did she believe that she should. Protect them, she would try. And pray for them. They were already blessed, she knew, simply by the fact that they were home alive, that their hearts were now in the right place, and out of the evil hands of Arriquibar Sosa.

Any traveler arriving at Bahía Kino was told that the town was owned by Arriquibar Sosa. They also said that he owned the waters, the mountains, the beauty of Tiburón Island, and the admirable sunset that cascaded across the Sea of Cortez and into the estuary of the mainland. But it was only the newest residents of this coastal town that talked about Sosa. The Seri people, who inhabited the land long before the Spanish made their presence, made no mention of him. They only knew of the land and the sea, that *they* were the great providers, and bore more power than any man.

Nonetheless, Sosa established his post, in a mass of adobe dwellings in the center of Bahía Kino, many for his *policía,* and for their women, but especially the *cantina,* which was a meeting place for many things, but most importantly, between his men and the men of the sea — the smugglers who brought him much needed supplies, especially now, guns and ammunition from the north.

Raul Vázquez was known as Sosa's hawk. A *jefe,* a colonel, Vázquez ran the town. He reported directly to Sosa, and answered only to his orders. They came to him by military couriers, usually a lieutenant, who led military parties, large and small, back and forth from Hermosillo. Sosa's words, on parchment, folded twice and with his own red wax seal, Vázquez had received many weeks ago, telling him that the incoming shipment was very important. Even though Vázquez knew nothing of the vision, or the military strategy behind it, he acted upon Sosa's orders without question.

The *jefe* was allowed only twenty-five men to help guard his city. Though they were thought of as *policía,* they were ranked like military. Three were lieutenants that reported directly to him, one sergeant, and twenty-one *soldados.* One of those was a teenage boy who also reported to him and was his local courier.

The only time there were more *policía* in Bahía Kino was when a shipment was expected. Sosa would send a detachment of ten to twenty men on the two-day, 110 kilometer trek across the desert to the port city. These men were mostly *soldados,* led by a colonel, captain, or lieutenant, and sometimes, if they expected there might be trouble, men from Sosa's elite, with their red and white arm bands. Vázquez knew nothing more than that these men were either expert marksmen, or expert fighters, or both. He liked it better when the leader of the detachment was a lower rank, because for some reason he did not feel as though someone else was running the town in his stead. But, truthfully, it did not matter, because regardless of who Sosa sent, due to the mission that they were on, it might as well be Sosa himself.

Though he was most commonly known solely as "the smuggler," his name was Boles. Whenever he was in Mexico it was a frustrating situation for Boles, because the Spanish speaking people didn't realize the "e" at the end of his name was silent. "Bol-ez," many of them would say, when it was supposed to be more like "Bolz," with the long "o" just as the Spanish speaking people pronounced it. And the worst problem was, once one person started the mispronunciation, that's the way it spread throughout the town. He was tired of correcting them, but once he got paid, he quickly got over it.

"Where is Bol-ez," were the words from Lieutenant Jesus Hilario after he walked into the *cantina.* Vázquez was happy to see the lieutenant with only ten *soldados* and none of Sosa's elite men, which meant they likely expected no trouble. Though the lieutenant saluted Vázquez upon his entrance, he still spoke to him as if he were no one to be questioned, and Vázquez knew better than to challenge him.

"He is down the street. With a *puta,* and probably drunk."

"Well," the lieutenant said, "sober him up. Sosa wants the guns immediately."

Vázquez nodded, and the lieutenant followed him out of the cantina and down the street to another adobe, where from outside they could hear laughing, singing, and music from an accordion. Vázquez knocked on the door, but the lieutenant quickly intervened, brusquely pushed his way ahead and opened the door. The music stopped and Boles, completely naked, jumped up from a mat on the floor. Two naked women — one on each side of him — screamed, grabbed for blankets and lifted them over their breasts. Vázquez acknowledged the older, bare-chested man who sat on a chair and held the accordion. Though Boles was annoyed at first, his demeanor quickly changed and he found a slight smile inside his sweaty, sunburned face and gray beard. He lifted a clear bottle of tequila and laughed. "Greetings, *caballeros.* Join me for a drink!"

The lieutenant looked around the room with a slight scowl. "I am not here for a drink and you know it."

Boles scratched the pale, freckled skin of his chest then took another drink. After he swallowed, and wiped his lips with his forearm, he nodded. "All right." He set the empty bottle on a near table then traipsed naked across the room where his trousers hung over the back of an empty chair and wasted no time putting them on.

"Where are the guns?" the lieutenant asked.

Boles gurgled a mess of phlegm in his throat then coughed it up and spat it on the floor. "On my boat, in the harbor."

"Very well," the lieutenant said. "We will meet you at our normal meeting spot."

Boles finished buttoning his shirt then pulled the braces from his pants over his shoulders. "You're gonna be waiting a while. My men still have to load the crates onto the raft, and navigating that thing through the bay and into that boggy lagoon. It's a good day's work. So hold on to your ass there *compadre,* and don't forget, I get my first half on arrival, the second half on delivery."

The lieutenant didn't skip a beat. "I will travel to your boat to confirm arrival, and there I will give you the $1,000 in gold."

"One thousand?" Boles said, with a sudden look of discontent. "The deal was for $3,000. Unless they do sums differently in Mexico, half is $1,500."

The lieutenant stood firmly, his face deadpan. "Señor Bol-ez, $1,000 each for three Civil War era Gatling guns, which no doubt have already been used in battle, is hardly a bargain."

Boles looked directly at Vázquez. "Who is this coyote?" He pointed a finger at the lieutenant. "It's 'Bolz,' goddammit . . . and you listen here. You either pay me what was agreed on or I get back on that boat and sail further south and sell them to the Mexican army for twice that much."

Vázquez held up a hand to Boles. "Wait a

minute, *señor.*" He turned his attention to the lieutenant. "I need to see you outside."

"I am only doing as instructed."

"Outside lieutenant!"

Though he did not rush to his command, Lieutenant Hilario followed Vázquez out the door and into the street where the waning sunlight cast its evening shadows on the tiny port town. When they had made several steps into the dusty street, Colonel Vázquez turned to face the lieutenant. "I know what you're doing."

Hilario stood poker faced and did not respond.

"Yeah, you're trying to pocket a grand in gold. You're forgetting, lieutenant, that I have a piece of parchment in there with Sosa's seal that specifically states this deal is for $3,000 in gold, half on arrival, and half on delivery."

"So what you are saying, is that you need your share."

Vázquez nodded. "The thousand you are pocketing . . . I want half."

Hilario smirked. "I figured as much, colonel. Do not worry, you will get your share."

Vázquez studied Hilario's eyes a moment. "All right, I am going with you onto the boat."

"As you wish, colonel." The lieutenant said then turned and walked away.

Emanuela stood at Enrique's bedside, holding his hand tightly, and looking tenderly into his eyes. Enrique lay there, bare-chested, with a large white bandage that wrapped around his armpit and over his shoulder several times. A blood spot about the size of a silver dollar had soaked through the center of the bandage.

"I was so worried about you," Emanuela said.

"Do not worry," Enrique said. "The bullet went in and out, and the doctor said it barely missed my collar bone. He said that I will have some tenderness for a while, but should heal fast. He also said I was lucky."

"We are all very grateful for your bravery." Emanuela turned her head and Amado, Felipe, and Javier all came forward and stood next to her.

Enrique smiled as he looked up at them. "I am so glad you are here, and safe. It brings me great joy."

The boys all smiled shyly.

Felipe's eyes brightened. "When you heal, Señor Enrique, will you teach us how to shoot the bow and arrow?"

"Si," Enrique said. "It is a promise to all

of you."

Emanuela put a hand over Felipe's mouth. "Do not bother Enrique with such things right now. He needs to rest."

"No," Enrique said. "It's quite all right."

At that moment Constanza walked into the room, came up behind the boys and looked over their shoulders. "How is our patient doing?"

"I am fine, *señora,*" Enrique said. He reached his right arm over to a bed stand and grabbed an amber colored bottle, topped with a porcelain stopper, and brought it to him. "I am very grateful for this medicine. Whenever I am hurting, it takes the pain away very quickly, and I feel very relaxed."

Constanza jerked the bottle away from him. "You must be very careful with this. It is opium, and too much can be worse than none at all."

Enrique smiled. *"Si, señora."*

Constanza set the bottle back down on the table and then turned to Emanuela. "Please, join us for supper in the dining room." She put her arms around Javier and Felipe. "And all you boys come, too. I want to celebrate your return to us."

Emanuela smiled and rubbed a hand through Amado's hair. "We would love to."

Constanza looked at Enrique. "I am also looking forward to meeting your American friend."

"Si," Enrique said. "He is a very good friend."

Pang, Sereno, and Dutton met Constanza and Jose and the rest of the dinner guests in the main dining room. After they sat around the table, and were served their dinner of *barbacoa de borrego* with chili sauce, bread, and avocados, with wine to drink, milk for the boys, they listened to Chas Dutton tell about his long travels from his home in Missouri all the way to Hermosillo.

"What is it like in Missouri?" Emanuela asked.

"Right now," Dutton said, "very cold, and snow up to your knees."

"Snow?" Amado said. "I have never seen snow, except on top of the mountains. Are there mountains in Missouri?"

"No, not in my part of Missouri. And not like the mountains you have here, anyway. Compared to here, they're more like mole hills."

Constanza raised her glass of wine. "I would like to make a toast to our American friend." They each raised their glasses in response. "To your health, Señor Dutton, and many thanks for your bravery today."

Dutton nodded, and they each took a sip from their glasses. The boys clinked their glasses of milk together and giggled. The rest of them joined in their laughter.

After they were finished eating, Constanza suggested Emanuela take the boys home and then she invited the men to meet her in her late husband's study for a nightcap, and something a little stronger than wine.

Emanuela agreed cordially, but before she could get the boys out of their chairs, Amado spoke up.

He looked directly at Constanza. "*Señora,* now that I am home, I have great fear for everyone here at the *hacienda.*"

Constanza drew a look of concern. "What is it, Amado?"

Amado glanced shyly around the table then looked back at Constanza. "I know that Sosa and his *policía* are planning an attack on the *hacienda.*"

"When?"

"I do not know," Amado said. "But I do know they are waiting on a new shipment of guns. Then they will attack."

Pang and Dutton also shared a look of grave concern.

"Guns?" Constanza said, looking down at the table in thought. She looked back up at

Amado with a look of disbelief. "They already have many guns. More than enough to take Sonora, let alone field workers on a *hacienda.*"

Dutton spoke up. "Ma'am, if I may?"

Constanza nodded. "Of course, Señor Dutton."

Dutton looked at Amado. "Do you know what kind of guns?"

"*Si,* Gatling guns. Three of them."

Everyone in the room shared looks of fear, but Dutton kept his eyes on the boy.

"Do you know where these guns are coming from?"

"They come from America, but they get them from a ship in Bahía Kino. There are men on their way now to get them."

Dutton looked at Pang. "Are you thinking what I'm thinking?"

Pang nodded, his face sober and composed. "I am with you."

Dutton looked at Constanza. "Ma'am, I think I'm ready for that drink in your study."

Darkness had set in over the bay by the time that Hilario and Vázquez reached the ship anchored a kilometer off shore from Bahía Kino. They rode in a skiff that easily sat six men, but there were only five of them, including Boles, and two of Boles men that navigated the small boat with oars.

They climbed aboard the ship by a rope ladder, and Boles led them across a deck by way of lantern light to three bundles, chest high and covered with tarps. When Boles' men removed the tarps, they revealed three square wooden crates, as wide as a buckboard wagon. The smuggler then instructed one of the men to open a crate, which then revealed what they all were after: the complete makings of a Gatling gun, mounted securely on an axel connected to two spoke wheels, and tongue for pulling which also substituted for a ground support when in use.

Hilario pointed toward the other crates. "Very well, let's see the others."

Boles' men wasted no time opening the other crates, and Vázquez walked along to each of the guns and tested the cranking handle, which rotated the ten barrels fluidly. Once satisfied, he looked at Hilario and nodded.

Hilario looked at Boles. "Ammunition?"

Boles led them to a longer and wider tarp-covered bundle, nearly stretching the full width of the ship. Boles' men removed the tarp to reveal several smaller boxes, each with latches and chest handles. Boles released one of the latches and opened the box.

"All .50 caliber," Boles said. "There are 400 in each box, and we have 50 boxes here. So that's 20,000 rounds."

Hilario and Vázquez both looked inside at the tarnished brass cartridges, and a long, brass stick magazine.

"I want to test one of the guns," Hilario said.

"Test?" Boles said. "On what?"

Hilario looked around for a moment, then pointed out into the darkness. "Not anything in particular. Just shoot it."

Boles shrugged, then nodded to his men. "As you wish."

In less then two minutes, Boles men had one of the guns wheeled to the side of the ship and pointed it west, and two other men carried an ammunition box and set it next to the gun. They attached the stick magazine into the feeder, then looked at Boles for further direction.

Boles nodded to Hilario and pointed a hand toward the crank handle. "Be my guest."

Hilario looked at Vázquez. "Colonel, would you like the honors?"

Vázquez glanced nervously at each of the men then stepped up to the back of the gun and grabbed on to the crank handle. He looked out into the night knowing that if the bullets had the range, they would hit somewhere on Tiburon Island, which was scarcely inhabited by human beings.

He rolled his fist forward and as quickly as he pushed the gun began firing, loud continuous blasts, sparks of fire, and empty brass cartridges ejecting at his feet as if all were one, harmonious symphony. He wasn't sure how many rounds he fired, since it all happened so quickly, but by the time they were all amassed in a cloud of smoke, he stopped cranking.

It took at least a minute for the smoke to clear the deck and for their ears to stop ringing, but it was clear to Vázquez that everything was in working order, and he nodded his approval to Hilario.

Hilario reached his leather satchel, which he carried by a thick strap that crossed his chest and rested on his shoulder, and retrieved three cloth bags. He handed them one at a time to Boles, who knelt down to the deck and one of his men came forward with a lantern. Boles opened each sack to confirm they were each filled with $20 gold pieces. It wasn't difficult for him to estimate that each sack held $500 in gold.

"That is your first half, Señor Bol-ez," Hilario said. "I trust now that you will arrange delivery to the cove."

Boles tied each bag shut, then stood back on his feet. "We will sail further down the harbor and get as close as we can to the cove. I have a raft down there, and we'll load all the crates on to it. Then we'll tow the raft with skiffs into the cove. There we can make the exchange."

"Very well," Hilario said. "I am ready."

Boles and his men went to work, raising the anchor and the sails, and he instructed his men to head toward the cove.

Hilario walked to the side of the boat and walked the deck all the way to the stern, where he grabbed a cigar out of his inside coat pocket, then lit it with a match and gazed out into the darkness. As he exhaled a large cloud of smoke he heard footsteps behind him and turned to find Vázquez. Once he acknowledged his presence Hilario turned away as if he wasn't even there.

Vázquez stood beside him. "What are you doing?"

Hilario glanced at the colonel but did not answer him.

"Answer me, goddammit. Why did you give him the full half?"

"I had to make sure we make it to the cove, first." The lieutenant looked back out into the darkness. "After we reach the cove, you will see that the gold Señor Bol-ez now has, is all he will ever see."

Chapter Nine

Behind the main house of *Hacienda de Ramírez* was a beautiful garden, decorated with palm trees, cactus, flowers, native rocks, and with a stone pathway that led to a wooden bench in the center of the garden. At every corner, and on every post, an oil lantern gave off just enough light to enjoy its beauty. Guadalupe Rojas sat there on the bench, with the poncho she had borrowed from the stable wrapped around her shoulders like a shawl. She stared into the garden, not really at anything in particular, but off in thought, about where she was now, how her life had led her to this moment, and about all of the uncertainty of her future.

Constanza Ramírez walked around the garden turning down the wicks of the lanterns, and eventually she saw Guadalupe sitting there. She refrained from her lantern duty and walked slowly to the center of the garden, where Guadalupe had already risen from the bench.

"I am sorry, *señora,*" Guadalupe said, turning away. "I will head in now."

"Wait," Constanza said.

Guadalupe stopped and turned back.

Constanza looked at her solemnly. "I want to thank you for what you did. It was brave of you, and you saved those boys' lives. I don't agree with what you do with your own life, but as long as you are free of it, you are welcome here."

Guadalupe lowered her head ashamedly. "If only you knew what it was like to live under Sosa's thumb. Whenever he has you, it never stops. You are never free again."

"You are right. I don't know what it's like." Constanza took a deep breath and let it out slowly. "There are many things in the world that I know nothing about. But one thing is for certain, no man has ever taken as much from me . . . everything that I ever loved, more than Arriquibar Sosa."

Guadalupe found a slight smile. "You see, whether you realize it or not, we have a little in common."

"How so?"

"I was once in love. I was very young girl . . . only fourteen. By the time I was fifteen I was pregnant, and I had to run away with him before my father killed us both. We ran away from our village south of here to Hermosillo. We got married in the church, by a real priest, and my husband started asking about work. That was when we met Arriquibar Sosa. He was just starting out as a trader . . . of cigars, wine, tequila, and even whiskey from America. My husband went to work for him, at first loading and unloading wagons. Before long he was driving the wagons, and then promoted to a *jefe* over all of the drivers and warehouses. We were so happy, with a new baby, and making a good living for being so young. But one night the fairytale life all came to an end."

"What happened, my dear?"

Guadalupe looked up, tears welled in her eyes and dripped down her cheeks. "My husband was working late, and Sosa came to our house with two of his bodyguards. At first I thought something was wrong with my husband, but soon I realized that they were there for other reasons."

"Oh no," Constanza said, grabbing hold of Guadalupe's hands.

"He forced himself on me while his two bodyguards held me down. One of them held a hand over my mouth to muffle my screams. My baby boy, he was crying, but I could not get to him. All I could think about was Sosa finishing so it would be over. But that wasn't enough for him." Now she looked directly at Constanza, anger shining through all of her sorrow. "He took my baby. He told me that if I ever wanted to see it again, that I had to do exactly as he said."

"What did you do?"

"I became his personal whore. My baby was kept by a nanny and I was allowed to see him once a day. And Sosa made sure I never saw my husband again."

"That is horrible. Do you know what became of your husband?"

"He kept working for Sosa, and after a couple of years I started to hear about him. He'd gotten over it, I guess. I grew to be very angry at him, but in time I realized he was as trapped as I was. He moved up in the ranks with Sosa, and several years later, he went to work for you."

Constanza was stunned by her statement. "For me? Who?"

"Fernando Jiménez."

Constanza's mouth fell agape and she was lost for words.

Guadalupe smiled disingenuously. "That's right, it was all part of Sosa's big plan to take over Sonora. Every business would pay him taxes, and if they did not, he took them over by whatever means necessary. May your dear husband rest in peace, *señora*. Santiago Ramírez was one of many who resisted, and one of many who died trying."

Constanza had to sit down on the bench to gather her wits. "There is no end to his evil. He must be stopped."

"I wish I had had this courage when I was younger. But I found it easier just to go along with it. My baby was everything to me. I couldn't bear not seeing him. But just last year he died. He was only twelve years old. Working as a courier for Sosa. Now I have nothing to lose."

Constanza grabbed her hand again and pulled her toward the bench, and Guadalupe sat down beside her.

"I can't imagine the pain you have been through," Constanza said. "But you are right. We have both lost so much, and I think that it is God's will that we now have each other."

They gripped each other's hands firmly and Guadalupe fell into Constanza's embrace and wept. Though Constanza held her tightly, and permitted her the time to release her emotions, Guadalupe wouldn't allow it to go on for long and stood up straight wiping at her eyes.

"You are so much stronger than me," Guadalupe said. "Of anyone in this world, I admire you the most."

"My dear, you have been so alone through all of this. You did what you did for your son. And there is great honor in that. Because of you now, I will never judge anyone in such a manner as I did you. I feel very blessed to have you here in my home, and to have heard your story. I feel as though the breath of God has just entered my lungs."

Guadalupe smiled, and then looked gravely at Constanza. "What are you going to do?"

"We have the blessing of *El Trio* now, and with God on our side, many miracles can happen."

"I gave up praying a long time ago, but now I will certainly pray that you are right."

It was almost daylight by the time the ship reached the mouth of the estuary, and Colonel Vázquez insisted they wait until nightfall to unload the cargo. Lieutenant Hilario argued that Sosa would not stand for the delay, but the colonel was quick to counter.

"It's too dangerous in the daylight. Sosa would execute both of us if he lost these weapons to some rogue thief or detachment of *federales*. We have no choice but to wait."

"Only because you outrank me will I agree to your orders, and that will be my defense should Sosa interrogate me."

Vázquez let it end at that, and though he wanted to go to the shore, to Bahía Kino, Hilario did not trust Boles enough to leave his sight without seeing the guns unloaded. Because of this fear, both men stayed on the boat the rest of the day, listening to accordion music, drinking American whiskey, and playing cards with the ship's mates. Hilario did not participate as much, only taking an occasional drink, and pacing the deck of the ship, occasionally inspecting the cargo as if it might disappear.

Right before dusk Boles sent two of his men out in a skiff to a dock at Bahía Kino after the raft boat, a sixty-foot, flat-bottomed vessel designed specifically to take cargo into shallow areas. Boles had already made arrangements with Vázquez to procure a navigator and two rowing men who knew the cove's safest waterways, free of snags and sandbars, and where they could dock and unload the guns and ammunition onto six buckboard wagons awaiting their arrival.

Hilario was starting to get nervous, pacing the deck of the ship as the night grew long, when finally a lantern could be seen on the waters, and within a few minutes the raft boat appeared and was tied from bow to stern to the side of the ship. Boles' crew lowered each of the crates down on pulleys, and it took half of the night to get everything secure. The navigator of the raft complained that the load was too heavy, that they'd never get to the dock without dragging bottom. When he suggested they take the cargo in two separate loads, Hilario jumped in adamantly against it.

"I will not stand for any more delays!" Hilario barked.

Boles grunted. "If that raft can't make it to the dock, then you'll face a delay much worse than taking it in two loads."

"He is right," Vázquez said. "We cannot take the chance."

Hilario glared at the colonel. "We are already way behind schedule because of your suggestions, and I will not listen to any more of them!" The lieutenant turned back to Boles and pointed toward the cove. "The whole load, *ahora*!"

Boles raised his eyebrows and shrugged. "Okay . . . on one condition."

"Who are you to be making conditions?"

Boles took two steps closer to Hilario and looked sternly at him. "Unless you're forgetting, Lieutenant, I am responsible for this load until it's put into your hands. And I am telling you that if we get into that cove and that raft bottoms out on a sandbar, *that* is the point of delivery and I take my payment. You want it your way then you have to complete the deal."

Hilario spoke through gnashed teeth. "You will get your payment, Señor 'Bol-ez,' now get that damned raft into the cove!"

Boles threw daggers with his eyes, and stepped within inches of the lieutenant and breathed his hot, stagnant breath into his face. "It's *Bolz,* goddammit. You call me 'Bol-ez' one more time and you're swimming back to shore. Now get out of my goddamn way and let me do my job."

With only periodic breaks to rest their horses, Dutton and Pang rode virtually nonstop, following the well-traveled road west from Hermosillo toward the desert flats outside the coastal town of Bahía Kino. Though they started out riding at night, when daylight came they put out their lanterns and spurred their horses to a lope. They had ridden for nearly six hours when they came across an elderly man, wearing a broad sombrero and a poncho, and pulling a burro that was attached to a two-wheel cart. He was going in the opposite direction, back toward Hermosillo, and when they passed him it was easy to see that the cart was empty. Dutton slowed his horse to a near stop and Pang followed suit. Dutton turned back and rode up to the old man. "*Con permiso, señor.* Can you tell me how much farther to Bahía Kino?"

When the man turned his head upward it was somewhat alarming to see that the irises of both his eyes were burdened with cataracts.

"If I told you how far, would that help you get there any quicker?"

Dutton leaned forward in his saddle, tipped his hat back and raised his eyebrows. "No, don't reckon it would."

"This place where you are going, you will find danger. Do not wish for it to happen, it will happen soon enough."

Dutton wrinkled his brow and offered a quick glance at Pang. "I suppose you're right about that, too. I'm sorry if we burdened you."

"You were no more of a burden than the dust I breathe from many travelers by, or the times my burro stops to relieve himself. We share this world, and we must accommodate each other."

"Gracias, señor." Though a bit perplexed

by this dialogue, Dutton couldn't help but feel a bit of sorrow for the old man. "*Señor,* can I offer you a drink from my canteen?"

The old man nodded. "Water is as important as the sun, though they are fierce competitors."

Dutton stepped down from his horse and carried the canteen over to the man, removed the cork, and held the spout up to the old man's lips. He responded by opening his mouth slightly and tipping back his head. Dutton poured the water slowly, and when the old man had his fill, he lowered his head and closed his mouth.

Dutton half smiled and put the cork back in the canteen. "I guess we'll be riding on."

As Dutton turned to walk back to his horse, he stopped when the old man spoke again. "This treasure that you look for, it is not the treasure you will find."

Before Dutton had any time to absorb what he said, or even respond, the old man started walking forward with his donkey and cart, and when Dutton had mounted his horse, and looked back once more, the old man was gone.

When they arrived at their destination, they were bone tired, and their hips sore from so much riding, but they knew they had to keep on with the mission. It was after midnight when they found the tracks that they were looking for, leading southwest off of the main trail. After their dinner with Constanza Ramírez and their meeting in her study, Constanza unrolled a map on a table and showed them where she believed they would meet. It all made sense, due to Amado's mention of smugglers on a ship, and a place to unload the shipments where no one would see them.

When they rode off of the trail, with only the dim lights of lanterns, and the stars in the sky and the horses' natural senses to guide them, Pang assured Dutton that they were in the right place. "I would know that smell anywhere. The smell of the sea makes its presence known in many ways, and where the waters of the rivers meet the salt waters of the ocean, it is a smell that one never forgets."

"I can certainly smell it," Dutton said, patting his mare on the neck. "And apparently this ol' girl can too."

"The question is, where do we go now?"

Dutton held his lantern over the ground to his right, and waved it around examining the trail. "It certainly looks like an army rode through here. Hard to tell how many riders. Looks like as many as six or eight wagons. It's serious business all right." He sat up straight and held the lantern head-high and peered ahead. "I say we walk these horses slowly, get off and lead them, and keep our eyes out for other lantern or fire light. That way we don't move too fast and have a chance to spot them before they spot us."

In agreement Pang dismounted and they each led their horses forward, carrying the lanterns at their sides. Pang looked farther out into the darkness, his head high, absorbing the sights and sounds ahead of them. Dutton paid more attention to the ground, waving the lantern over the tracks, making sure they stayed on the trail. After they had walked at least two miles, eventually he saw where the trail veered back toward the northwest.

Pang followed his lead for another quarter mile and then he stopped, and whispered to Dutton to do the same.

"Hear that?" Pang said.

Dutton listened carefully. "Yeah, I hear voices."

They both looked straight west into the night.

"Over there," Pang said, pointing in the same direction. "I also hear the lapping of water."

"But I don't see anything," Dutton said. "Not even a hint of a light."

"Then we must be very careful," Pang said. "I will turn my lantern out. You lower the light on yours and keep us on the trail, and I'll keep listening."

The farther they walked, the louder the voices became. Eventually Pang saw a faint image of light, and got close enough to Dutton to tug on his arm. He pointed straight ahead and spoke in a whisper. "There, maybe a hundred yards, see it?"

Dutton's eyes rotated inside their sockets looking for Pang's discovery, and finally they locked on. "Yeah, I see it. Looks like light in a tent."

"Exactly. We should find a place to tie our horses now, and move in on foot."

"There won't be anything here, unless we can find a willow or something to tie to. We best just tie the horses together, and I've got some hobbles in my saddlebags."

"Very well."

"But I have another concern," Dutton said, turning his head to the left and right.

"What?" Pang said.

"They surely have men posted out here somewhere, guarding their trail."

"But we would have run into them by now."

"Yeah, that's what worries me."

They led the horses off the trail and Dutton retrieved the hobbles. Dutton made sure both of his .45 Colts were secure in their holsters, and then grabbed his Winchester rifle from its scabbard.

Just as they felt ready to move forward, a bright light sparked only ten feet in front of them. As the light dimmed, they saw the glow of their faces — three uniformed guards, two holding guns, and the one in the center with a lit match that he applied to a lantern wick. The men at his side each aimed their rifles from their sides.

"Who are you?" the man with the lantern said.

Dutton cleared his throat and Pang was glad he decided to do the talking. "I am a marine detective, and I was sent ashore to find an escaped slave." Dutton put a hand on Pang's shoulder. "Finally found this coolie here out wandering in the desert. *Loco* bastard, wouldn't you say?"

Pang looked at Dutton with a perplexed gaze.

The soldier held the lantern higher and peered over at the horses. "If this is true, then why are your horses tied?"

"Well," Dutton said. "We've almost reached shore, and we decided to camp here until morning."

The man studied him a few seconds before saying anything more. "There is no dock in this direction. Why are you camped here off of the main trail?"

"Well now, what would you do if you were a gringo traveling with a Chinaman? Feller can't get in a good *siesta* while he's worrying about someone coming down the trail in the middle of the night. Now am I right?"

The man was slow to respond, but he finally nodded. "*Si,* I understand. But you better not camp here. Come in to our camp so others know about you and there are no more surprises."

Dutton laughed. "Ain't that the truth! We don't like too many surprises, especially this time of night."

The man nodded toward the horses. "Bring your horses, and follow us."

Dutton glanced at the horses, then back at the men very quickly. "Say, speaking of these horses, can you help hold them while I remove the hobble?" He laughed again. "You know these Chinamen. They don't know a goddamn thing about horses and tack."

The man nodded and the other two lowered their weapons and stepped closer. Once Dutton was behind the shadow of his horse, he made eye contact with Pang, who had turned his back to the men, and nodded as if now he understood. When the men were close enough, Pang swung around and kicked the lantern out of the man's hand and sent it flying into the air. It all happened so quickly and caught them so surprised that pivoting around and taking a gun from one, then striking the other, was done with precision timing.

Dutton stepped out from behind the horse, revolver drawn, and cocked back the hammer. "Okay, amigos. Let's put those guns on the ground. I don't like killing, but I've done it before, and I'll do it again if I have to."

The soldiers were hesitant, but they did so by the persuasion of their leading officer.

Pang grabbed some rope and followed them off the trail as Dutton held them at gunpoint. The Chinaman tied each of their hands behind their backs, then all three of them back-to-back, with a rope around their shoulders at the biceps. He also removed each of their khaki neckerchiefs and made gags by tying them from inside their mouths to the back of their heads. Dutton held the lantern up higher so Pang could inspect all of his knots, and each of the Mexican soldiers looked up at him with wide-eyed fear.

"Y'all don't worry none," Dutton said. "Being where you are now gives you a better chance at living than most of the other men we'll meet tonight. So relax, stay calm, and think about your future, because you might actually have one."

Though they knew it wouldn't be easy to see without one, they decided to put the lanterns out and leave them near the horses. At this moment carrying a lantern would do nothing more than get them noticed, and that they didn't want. It was very likely that that was how the three men they'd just tied up noticed them. They felt lucky they weren't shot first, and only inquired, and had the chance to stay on their mission.

They moved slowly, kept their eyes on that glowing spot of light inside a tent, and before long they noticed three other tents and a campfire, which had died down to mere glowing embers. They stopped a good thirty yards from the closest tent, crouched down and listened.

"I think the camp is abandoned," Pang said.

"Not abandoned," Dutton said. "Just not occupied at the moment. I'd say them fellers back there were the ones on duty to protect it."

"If that is the case, then where are the other men?"

Dutton scanned the area and almost instantly he saw a glimmer of light, a good hundred yards out, and pointed in that direction. "There. It looks to be in the water."

"Where do you suppose the guns are?"

"I don't know," he said, now pointing back into the camp. "But I can see wagon wheels over there. Let's work our way in that direction and inspect the cargo."

The two men crouched carefully through the camp, peeking inside each of the tents to make sure they were correct about it not being occupied. It was just as Dutton had figured, all of the tents were empty, and no one else in sight.

Though they were not sure how many guns were on this shipment, they counted eight wagons, each connected to two draft horses. Six of the wagons were completely filled with wooden boxes that had metal handles on each side. Pang unlatched and felt inside one of the boxes and was certain that the content was ammunition. He heard a whistle, and looked to see the faint image of Dutton waving for him. Pang crouched down and shuffled over to Dutton, who lit a match, and before them, by the glow of the burning flame, was the Gatling gun, just as Amado had described, mounted on axels and spoke wheels just like a cannon, and the tongue attached to a doubletree at the back of the wagon.

"Haven't seen one of these since the war," Dutton said. He raised the match higher and looked behind him at the adjacent wagon. "And there's another one."

"Are they dangerous?"

Dutton grunted. "The only way to beat one is to be equally matched, and hope you're the one left with bullets."

Pang nodded toward the empty wagons. "It appears there is one more?"

"Yeah, by my calculation, they brought just enough wagons for three guns, and enough ammunition to start a war."

"Do we wait?"

Dutton peered out to the lantern ahead, that seemed to be getting closer. "I say we go ahead with our plan — with what is already here, and then wait for the rest of the party."

They had talked through their plan most of the way from Hermosillo, especially at night when they couldn't ride as fast. Though they weren't sure in what order it would all go down, they decided to go ahead and get as many boxes of ammunition as would fit in a wagon, with the gun towed behind, and get that wagon safely out of camp. They could only fit ten boxes on the wagon, and that was after the tailgate was removed, which caused them to hang over the end a good foot and a half. Dutton found some rope and crossed it over the ends of the boxes and tied it to the sides of the wagon, which would lessen the chance of the boxes bouncing and sliding out.

When everything was secured to his liking, he jumped up on the seat, snapped the reins, and drove the wagon all the way back to where their horses were tied. He quickly removed the hobbles and tied the horses to the wagon, which ensured they'd be ready when it came time to leave. Though they wouldn't be able to make a quick departure with the wagon, anything that saved time was of the essence at this moment.

Pang began his part of the plan by grabbing an ammunition box and carrying it to the water. It was very heavy, but his father had taught him how to use his legs and hold such heavy objects, and the handles on each end made it much easier. He kept a watchful eye on the lantern light ahead, and though it did appear to be getting closer, it was certainly at a slow pace. When he reached the bog he set the box on end into about a foot of water. He opened the latch and pulled back the lid until all of the cartridges fell into the water and completely disappeared.

By the time Dutton returned, he brought with him two wooden bowls that he found in the camp. Pang nodded his agreement that they would work well with their plan. For the time being Dutton helped him drag the rest of the ammunition out into the shallow water, dumping the contents, all but the magazines, which Dutton stuck down behind his belt and carried back with him.

"Why are you keeping those?" Pang asked.

"Because you can have all the Gatling guns and ammunition you want, but they won't work very well without these."

"But we are getting rid of the ammunition."

Dutton nodded then looked out toward the lantern flicking off shore. "But we don't know that we got all of it."

When they had emptied all of the ammunition boxes, they took the bowls to the nearest point on the shore and scooped up as much mud as would fit in the bowl. They each carried the bowl back to the gun and Dutton proceeded to fill the breech opening with the wet, sandy sludge, then dipped some of it out with his fingers and stuck it up inside the ejector opening. Once he felt it was enough, he grabbed the crank handle and he barely made one rotation before the crank would no longer turn.

"That should do it," he said. "That gun is officially out of commission." He tossed the bowl down on the ground and peered out into the darkness of the estuary. He could now see three lights instead of one, and they were much closer.

"What do we do now?" Pang said.

Dutton took a deep breath and thought for a moment. "If there's another gun out there, we've got to disable it."

"How are they getting them ashore?"

Dutton walked to the back of the wagon, squatted, and pointed toward the ground. He lit a match and Pang looked over his shoulder. "See here," he pointed a finger over a wide, smooth track. "These are from runners. Kind of like a sled. They are getting them as far as they can by boat, and then pulling them here the rest of the way." Both men stood back up and looked out toward the lights. "That's why they're moving so slow."

Suddenly Pang pointed toward the smallest light. "Look, only two of them are coming closer, the other is farther out."

"Yeah, that would be their boat. And the other two lights are guiding the poor bastards that have to wade through the sludge."

"Maybe it would be easier to fight them out there, and dump the gun and ammunition off into the muddy water? It would be better than waiting until it was here to disable it."

Dutton looked perplexed at the Chinaman. "You want to wade out there in that mud?"

"Back in China, my father gave me many kung fu lessons in the paddy fields. We stood in water and were not allowed to use our feet, only our hands as defense. It taught us balance and focus."

"But you got to remember, those *hombres* have guns."

"Yes, but they are busy holding ropes and lanterns. I will sneak up on them like a serpent and they will never know what hit them."

Dutton pondered Pang's idea. "All right, since I'd be worthless as tits on a boar hog fighting in mire, I'll sit right here on this wagon and keep my rifle sights on that boat light, just in case they cause you any trouble."

Pang nodded. "Yes, that is good. You are

good with guns, so that is the best place for you."

Dutton got on his knees behind the ammunition boxes and rested his rifle on top, pointing it out toward the distant light.

Pang took off his already muddy boots and tossed them in the wagon, then rolled up his trouser cuffs to just below the knee. "That should do it."

Dutton smirked at the Chinaman. "If you find the time, bring me back a nice halibut."

Pang smiled and offered a slight bow, then turned and tiptoed through the soft sand and disappeared into the darkness.

Three soldiers waded in the bog and helped one of Boles' men lower down the last of the ammunition boxes off of the sea raft and onto their makeshift sled, which was originally an eight foot raft only now built on smooth timbers that served as runners. The sled rested on top of a sandbar, with its tail dipping into the shallow marsh. Two of the soldiers got a hold of the lead ropes, which were made into loops and tied to the front corners of the sled. They wrapped the looped ropes around their chests and pulled like mules, while the other soldier stepped in front of them leading the way with a lantern.

Boles looked back at Hilario and Vázquez and brushed his hands together. "Well, that does it. Time to pay up."

Rather than retrieve the bags of gold from his shoulder bag, Hilario pulled out a revolver, pointed it at Boles and cocked the hammer. He nodded toward Boles' shipmate and motioned with the gun for him to back up.

Boles stared back in surprise. "What the hell is this?"

Hilario half smiled and took two steps backward. "This is where you abandon ship, Señor 'Bol-ez'."

Boles looked at Vázquez. "You agree with this?"

Vázquez could not look Boles in the eye, and said nothing.

Hilario waved the tip of the six-gun in a circular motion. "But before you go anywhere, I want you to retrieve those bags of gold from your pockets and drop them on the deck."

Boles pinched his lips. "So that's how it is, eh? You following orders here Hilario? Or is this just some little side bet you have with yourself?"

"This is no bet," Hilario said, followed by a smile. "This is a sure thing."

Boles glared at Hilario, but did as he said

and retrieved the leather bags and dropped them down on the raft deck.

"Good," Hilario said, tilting his head sideways. "Now, get off the boat. You can walk to shore. Your man here is going to take us to the dock."

"You think you're smart, but I promise you Sosa is going to hear about this."

Hilario lost his smug grin. "Get off the boat, now!"

With a slight hesitation, Boles walked across the swaying deck to the edge, then jumped down into the knee deep water, his feet sinking into the thick silty bottom.

Hilario motioned to the shipmate with a sideways nod, but kept his gun pointed at Boles. "Push off . . . let's get going."

Rather than walk toward the shore, Boles stood there in the bog, glaring up at Hilario as the shipmate pushed with an oar and the raft drifted away.

Suddenly Hilario started laughing, and he extended his arm and pointed the gun directly at Boles. "And here is why Sosa will never hear a word from you."

The gun blast echoed across the still waters and sent Boles flying backward to a splashing landing. Hilario turned quickly as the shipmate jumped into the water on the other side of the boat. He dived down and tried to swim away, but it was too shallow for him to gain any quick distance, and all Hilario had to do was point and shoot — ending it all with two quick shots and a hearty laugh. He turned back toward his men, who glared back at him with fear and confusion. "Well, what are you doing just standing there?" He pointed northeast toward the shore. *"Vayamos!"*

Chapter Ten

This was a job for Sosa's elite, which was why he gave it to his number one. Chavón brought two men from the special squad, though not according to number, but by skill. These two, known only to Sosa as number nineteen and number twenty-six, scored the highest in infiltration. They met at the headquarters, where he drew them a map of the *hacienda,* and the main *casa,* and since neither of them knew where Fernando would be hiding, they all knew that the best way to find him would be through interrogation.

They all three rode out to the *hacienda* in the middle of the night, and Chavón sent them in, across the darkness of the cotton field, dressed in dark clothing, and charcoal spread on their faces.

Though the guards were fairly easy to get by, they never calculated Sereno. The Tohono O'odham never slept in the same place twice, and even when he found a spot he liked, he rarely slept. His spot on this night was just inside the loft door of the stable, wearing a poncho to cut the chill, and peering out into the courtyard. Though there was not much to see in the darkness, under the lantern lights he could make detect a faint image of the two guards standing outside the main door of the *casa*. He quickly sat upright when he saw what looked like shadows running, and then he realized that two men, dressed in dark clothing, were running toward the *casa*.

Sereno jumped up and ran across the loft, climbed down the ladder, and when he reached the double doors of the stable, he looked out and saw the men again, creeping along the outside wall and heading toward the main door. The guards were oblivious to their presence, and though in such circumstances he would normally warn Enrique, he knew there was no time for that.

He moved as close to the *casa* as he could without the risk of being seen, and stopped and hid behind the circular stone wall around the water basin. He rubbed his hands along the ground and found several stones about the size of chicken eggs, and one at a time, tossed them toward the main opening. The guards saw them hit the ground in front of them, and after the initial confusion, they held their guns up and stepped farther out into the opening. They looked around, and eventually one of them saw the men and pointed.

"Who goes there?" He yelled.

The men turned to run, and then both of the guards saw them, aimed their guns and shot. One of the mysterious men fell, which caused the other to stop but he did not retreat and kept on running. The guards kept shooting, but to no avail. The man disappeared into the darkness over the cotton field.

The gunfire shook the people of the *hacienda* from their beds. They all ran into the courtyard and the two guards dragged the injured man to the main door.

He lay on the ground glaring up at Constanza, with a hand covering a bleeding wound in his hip, and the whites of his eyes very clear amidst the layer of charcoal on his face.

"Who are you?" Constanza said.

The man did not answer, but Guadalupe stood next to Constanza and looked down at him. "He's an assassin. He is one of Sosa's special brigade."

Constanza looked down on him in fear. "Assassin?" Her face turned to anger. "Who did you come here to kill?"

Again, the man did not answer, and only glared at her, then around at each of them.

"It was not you," Guadalupe said. "It was Fernando."

"Fernando?" Constanza said? "Why?"

"Because he is a traitor. Just like me. To Sosa the only punishment for such a thing is death."

The guards stood him up on his feet. One of them addressed Constanza. "What do we do with him, *señora*?"

Constanza looked him up and down. "Is he armed?"

The guard held up the man's pistol. "Not anymore."

"Then let him go. We take no prisoners here. But you come back and you will die."

"He will die anyway," Guadalupe said. "To Sosa, the other penalty of death is for failure."

The man continued to glare at them, and when the guards let loose of him he backed up then limped away.

Enrique stepped forward. "It is getting increasingly dangerous here. I am wondering if sending Pang and Dutton away was a good idea."

"No," Guadalupe said. "If they succeed, keeping those weapons out of the hands of

Sosa's men will be as good as cutting off all of their feet."

"I will pray then," Enrique said, "that they are victorious."

Constanza held Enrique's hand. "We all will pray."

Dutton could tell by the gun flashes that they took place near the farthest light. Three shots, he thought, which made him wonder if they spotted Pang and were shooting at him. He wasn't sure that not hearing any more was better or worse, but he also knew there was nothing he could do but keep his rifle pointed in that direction and stay calm.

After the echoes of the gunshots died out, the light on the boat started to move toward the sea, and eventually faded away. He now kept his sights on the other lights, and in the calm he heard voices and grunts, and was not sure what they were all about. With his adrenaline at a new high, all suddenly went silent. No voices, no grunts, save the distant lapping of the tide hitting the shore. Now he had fear for his friend, and that at any moment he might have to come up with a new plan.

When the water was deep enough, Pang back-floated toward the oncoming lights.

He kept his face above water just enough that he could breathe and keep a sidelong view of his destination. Eventually the reddish reflection of a large crate and the faces of four men came into view, with one in the lead holding the lantern and two others leaning forward and grimacing, as though they were laboring. The other man, the farthest back, crouched much lower, occasionally looking down, and his forehead glowed in the light. Pang quickly remembered what Dutton had said about the sleds, and the closer he got to the men, he realized that's exactly what they were doing — pulling a sled across the ridge of a sandbar.

Before Pang could make his move forward, he had to locate the other lights, and when he turned he easily found them, but suddenly there was distance growing between them. As he was calculating how to make his attack, a gun blast near the farthest light created a flash of light and caused everyone to stop. Pang's immediate thought was that they had spotted him, but without a light on him he quickly realized that was impossible. But what was happening? The light continued to move toward the west and two more continuous shots rang out. In the fading report of the gunfire, there was brief laughter, then yelling, and the language was easily discernable as Spanish.

Regardless of any imminent danger, Pang knew he had to proceed, or any delay might put Dutton and the entire plan in jeopardy. Being that he was sure that the crate before him now carried another Gatling gun, keeping it from reaching the shore, and disabling it, was the center of his attention.

He heard no more shots, and the light on the boat kept getting farther away, so he proceeded toward the men. The closer he got, the shallower the water became, and he decided to turn over and crawl slowly on his hands and knees up onto the sandbar. Though he kept a watchful eye on all of them, as well as the party that tailed them, his focus was on the man in the back. He circled slightly and came up from behind him, watching the soldier's feet dig deep into the sandbar as he leaned over and helped push the raft. Like a crab on a beach, Pang worked his way closer, slowly and quietly, and when the distance was adequate, the Chinaman reached forward with each hand and grabbed the man's ankles and jerked them back. The man grunted loudly and fell hitting his forehead on the raft, and when Pang turned him over, the man was out cold.

The noise caught the attention of the man

carrying the lantern, and he stopped and turned to look back, holding the lantern up as high as his head. *"Qué pasó?"*

Pang ducked down low and crawled back a few steps. After the soldier didn't get a response, he headed toward the back of the raft and the other soldiers stopped pulling. After the man stopped and shined the light over his unconscious comrade, Pang rose up and lunged forward and braced himself in front of the soldier in a broad stance. The wide-eyed soldier had no time to respond, as Pang grabbed the lantern with one hand, and punched the soldier's chest with the other. The soldier bent and wheezed, losing his breath, and then Pang, with his hand in a fist, knocked the man cold with a backward jab to the side of his head.

The Chinaman, lantern still in his left hand, jumped up on the raft, then to the top of the crate, and stood in a sprawling stance looking down on two glaring, astounded soldiers. They quickly let the tow ropes fall to the ground, but before they could react, Pang jumped down between them, jabbing both of their abdomens simultaneously with his elbows, which caused them both to buckle and groan. The final jabs to the head were then easy to instigate, and once Pang was sure that they were unconscious he turned to check on the other party behind him. Though they were still far enough back that he couldn't see their faces, nor count how many were there, he assumed there were at least four, and that he would have to act quickly to beat their arrival.

Pang set the lantern down on the deck of the small raft and with the base of his palms he pushed upward on the lid of the crate. Though it was slow to come off, once it was completely removed Pang retrieved the lantern and was not surprised to see another Gatling gun identical to the ones behind the wagons. He quickly jumped down and scooped up a handful of wet sand from the sandbar, and remembering what Dutton had done with the mud, he found the breach and ejector openings and filled them with the wet sand. He turned the crank handle until it would no longer turn. A sudden gun blast caused him to flinch, immediately followed by a bullet that splintered the edge of the crate.

Pang jumped down to the sandbar and hid behind the crate. Bullets continued to ricochet and thud in the sandbar around him.

"Ugh . . . I hate guns!" Pang said.

Suddenly he heard a gunshot from behind him, and turned and crawled backward against the crate. The shots continued to ring out, and in a matter of two seconds the faint glow of Dutton's face appeared and he jumped down next to Pang.

"Need some help there, amigo?" Dutton said.

Pang acknowledged Dutton's bare feet and trouser cuffs rolled up above the calf. Dutton stood up on his knees, laid the rifle over the crate, and fired three rapid shots, the empty cartridges ejecting onto Pang's lap. Gun smoke lingered around them as Dutton pulled the gun back down, retrieved bullets one at a time from his belt, and loaded ten into the breech. After all were loaded he pulled the lever, bringing a new bullet into the chamber, then rose back up and once again pointed the rifle over the crate. But he did not fire.

"There's no lantern light now," Dutton said. "Do you hear anything?"

Pang shook his head. "No. Do you think you got them?"

"I have no idea. They could have dropped the lantern in the fray and it went out." Dutton looked on the ground around him. "Looks like you got two of them taking a sand nap."

"Four."

"Four?"

"There are two more on the other side."

Dutton grinned. "Christ Almighty. Who needs a gun when you can have a Chinaman."

"Then maybe I should work my way around to check on them?"

Dutton nodded. "It sure worked once. Why not try it again?"

"But there is no light this time. How will I see them?"

Dutton peeked back over the crate. "Well, you're in luck. They've turned their lantern back on."

Pang looked over the crate as well. "Okay, I will call you when ready." As he scooted around to crawl into the water, he heard one of the soldiers moan. Pang looked back at Dutton. "If one of them tries to get up, try the neck pinch."

"Neck pinch?"

Pang put his hand around his own neck and right under his jaw. "Squeeze here, and it cuts off the blood to their brain and they pass out. It will buy you some time."

Dutton watched the Chinaman crawl away, and then looked back at the moaning guard. "Neck pinch?"

■ ■ ■ ■

"You are mad," Vázquez said, after Hilario had turned to face him. The sea raft slowly continued its course back out into the bay, but since the navigator was now dead in the water, someone else had to pick up the oar and assume his position. Hilario, with his gun now pointed at the colonel, decided that he was the best candidate.

"Colonel, if you want to live to see your half of that money, you better grab that damn oar and get us back to the main port, *ahora*!"

Vázquez looked at him with disgust, but finally picked up the oar, and instead of putting it into the water, he swung it upward, knocking the gun out of Hilario's hand, and then crossways at an upward angle hitting him under the chin. The lieutenant hit the deck hard, and Vázquez quickly picked up the gun.

Hilario lay there and moaned as the colonel grabbed some rope, then turned him over and tied his hands behind his back. To be sure he didn't run away when they hit shore, he also tied his feet together.

The colonel stuck the gun under the waist band of his trousers, then walked to the center of the sea raft and pulled on a small rope that released a sail. The light wind was just enough to allow the colonel to maneuver the small craft out of the cover and into the bay, then northwest toward the dock at Bahía Kino. It took nearly an hour to accomplish that short distance, and when the port light was in sight, he dropped the sail and used the momentum and the tail rudder to guide the boat toward the dock.

Two of his own men, who were on duty guarding the dock, were ready for him when he threw the rope and they pulled the raft in and tied it off to a dock post.

The colonel walked back over to Hilario, who still lay tied up on the dock, and reached inside his bag that lay next to him, and pulled out all of the bags of gold.

"Going to take it all for yourself now, eh colonel?"

Vázquez grabbed him by the back of the shirt collar and lifted him up on his feet. "No, you *and* the gold are going back to Hermosillo. The gold goes back to Sosa, and I'm sure you'll face the firing squad."

Vázquez whistled to the two guards to come aboard, and he reached down and untied Hilario's ankles. When the guards were there he grabbed Hilario by the arm and pushed him toward them. "Take him to the jail cell for the moment. I'll be there shortly to get him."

Before they led him away, Hilario grinned back at the colonel. "How do you know that I wasn't acting on Sosa's orders?"

"If that's the case, then I'm a dead man either way. So I'll take my chances that you're the lying bastard that you've proven to be."

Maneuvering through the marsh and back to the sandbar was a bit more nerve racking this time, since they already knew the enemy was there, but Pang was surprised to find that two of the soldiers lay motionless on the ground, and another sat up with his back against the raft, holding the lantern and breathing hard. After further inspection, he saw no more men and concluded there had been only three, unless one or more had run off. Regardless, he knew he had to be cautious.

As he had done before, he worked his way to the back, but this time crawled around the side toward the front, noticing that this particular raft carried only boxes of ammunition. When he peeked around to the front he could see that the solider sitting up was nursing a gunshot wound to his thigh. The two soldiers that had been pulling the ropes were laying face down, one with a bloody wound on his back, which had the appearance of an exit wound, and the other with one in the head. Confident they were dead, Pang decided to get up on his knees and peek over the boxes and try to get a better look at the man sitting up. But before he could make a move he heard a click, and looked up to find that solider laying down on his side and pointing his pistol directly at Pang. The man's forehead was covered with rivulets of sweat that glowed from the lantern light. He breathed heavily, which Pang presumed was caused by the pain from the wound.

Pang slowly raised his hands. "Hello, my friend. Please, I do not want to hurt you."

"No," the man said through clenched teeth. "You want to kill me."

Pang shook his head. "No, your men shot first. I do not even have a gun, see? My friend back there, he was only shooting back in self-defense."

"Friend? Back where?"

"At the other raft. He is waiting for my safe return."

The man squinted a bit. "Hey . . . I know who you are, you're one of *El Trio*!"

"El Trio? What is *El Trio?"*

The soldier shook his gun nervously.

"Don't you be joking with me! I know all about you . . . and that arrow fighter!"

Pang tried not to make it known that Dutton was sneaking up behind the man, tiptoeing in his bare feet, holding the rifle with both hands. When he was close enough, he reared back then struck the man on the back of the head with the butt of the rifle. The man fell cold.

Pang lowered his hands and took a deep breath, then crawled to the man and untied his neckerchief.

"What are you doing?" Dutton said.

"He has a bad wound on his thigh. I am making him a tourniquet bandage."

"Suit yourself. I had to use that neck pinch technique of yours on all four of those *hombres* back there. I was runnin' around like a coyote chasing a rabbit."

While Pang cared for the unconscious man, Dutton grabbed the lantern and inspected the boxes, and sure enough, all were full of ammunition. He opened them, and like before, removed the magazine clips and stuck them inside the waistband of his trousers, and when Pang was ready, they grabbed a handle on each end of the box and carried them out to the water and dumped them.

When they were through with the last box,

Dutton shook his head. "Such a waste, but then again, all you gotta do is think about the folks these bullets was meant for, and you'll know they are a lot better right where they're at."

Pang looked toward the east and pointed at the horizon. A hint of dark blue allowed a slight silhouette of the distant mountains. "Maybe now it's a good time to get out of here?"

Dutton nodded. "The sooner the better. We don't know who or what we might encounter on the way back."

When they got back to the wagon they checked on the men they'd tied up and all were leaning together asleep. Dutton kicked one of them in the foot which startled him enough to wake the others. Pang removed the gags and Dutton spoke.

"Now it wouldn't be humane to leave you boys like this, but we can't have you follerin' us neither. So, I'm sorry for having to do this."

Dutton and Pang both grabbed a neck and performed the pinch, and since Pang was a bit more experienced with the technique, Dutton allowed him to do the third man. When all three men had passed out, Pang untied their hands and feet while Dutton looked on.

He put his hands on his hips and shook his head while he looked over the unconscious men. "Neck pinch. I'll be goddamned."

A hazy dawn was upon them as Vázquez rode into camp with twelve of his own men following, and Hilario on a horse beside him with his hands tied together. The colonel acknowledged the tents, the horses and wagons loaded with cargo, and the men around the campfire that quickly stood to attention.

After Vázquez dismounted he looked back at his men. "I want all of you to dismount and come into the camp, and help these men tear down and prepare for the ride to Hermosillo." He looked directly at one of his lieutenants. "I want you to stay here with Hilario."

The lieutenant nodded and the rest of the men dismounted and followed Vázquez into the camp. The men in the camp all saluted the colonel, and he recognized some of them that had helped unload the sea raft, but they appeared battered and weary. He quickly counted eight men, and noted that one had a bloody wound on his thigh.

"Who's in charge here?" Vázquez said.

One of the men pointed at Hilario on the

horse. The colonel turned around to see Hilario smirking at him, and then turned back to all the men. "All right, I guess I am in charge now. I need someone to fill me in on the status of the cargo."

They all looked at each other, and finally the man with the wounded thigh spoke up. "It was *El Trio*!"

"El Trio? Who the hell is *El Trio?"*

"They are a legend . . . fighting men, but they are also thieves. They took one of the wagons, one of the guns, and ten boxes of ammunition."

The colonel let out a long breath. "Okay . . . so that leaves us with two guns and forty boxes of ammunition."

"No colonel."

"No?"

The wounded soldier looked around nervously. "Maybe you better come and see for yourself."

The man limped over to the wagons and he and the colonel both looked over the side rail at the many ammunition boxes and opened them.

"They are all empty, colonel," the man said.

"How could they steal it without the boxes?"

"They didn't steal it, colonel. They

dumped it." He pointed toward the cove. "Out there, in the water."

The colonel gazed out across the marsh and sandbars in disbelief. He pondered the situation a moment, and then looked over at the two other wagons. "The guns?"

"They are there, yes, but not in working condition."

"What do you mean?"

"I better show you."

The colonel walked behind the wagon and the soldier pointed at the breech opening.

"Mud," the soldier said. "In here and in the ejector opening. In both guns."

The colonel pinched his lips together and glanced down the line of wagons. "*Dios mio.* Sosa is going to be angry."

"*Si,* colonel," the wounded soldier said. "The guns can be cleaned, but it will require taking them completely apart, cleaning, oiling, and reassembling them. We have a gunsmith in Hermosillo that can do it."

Vázquez pondered the suggestion then nodded. "All right, let's take them there immediately. But I have to figure out the problem with the ammunition. Do you know where they dumped it?"

"We think that most of it was close to the wagons, depending on how far they dragged or carried the boxes. The others were out there on the raft. When we came to, we found the boxes empty."

"What do you mean 'came to'?"

The soldier looked around embarrassed. "*El Chino,* and the gringo, they knocked us out. And some of us . . . well, they pinched our necks."

"Pinched your necks?"

"*Si,* colonel. And the gringo, he shot and killed two men. I was the lucky one who was only wounded."

"Where are the bodies?"

"In the back of the empty wagon, colonel."

The colonel sighed. "All right, we'll take them back to their families."

"*Si,* colonel."

Vázquez shook his head in disbelief, and then turned to face all of the men. "All right . . . everyone, off with your boots and roll up your pants. I want you all to wade around out there and try to find as many of the cartridges as you can." The colonel clapped. "*Rápidamente!* Take an empty box with you. I will give you thirty minutes!"

All of the men did as the colonel said, but the wounded soldier was quick to brief him further. "Colonel?"

"What is it?"

"Even if we replaced the ammunition, we still don't have the magazines."

"Magazines. *Si,* that's right. I suppose they dumped them too?"

"I don't know, colonel."

Vázquez kicked at the ground. "Dammit!" The colonel also knew that he needed to send men after the ones who did this, but after seeing the condition of Hilario's detachment, he wondered how many he could spare. But who was this *El Trio*? A legend? What could three men do to an entire army?

Dutton drove the wagon, with his own horse tied behind next to the Gatling gun, and Pang rode a good half mile ahead of him. Occasionally Pang would find a high point where he could look in both directions for several miles, looking for oncoming danger. Encounters with the *policía* could come from any direction, and they had no doubt that, when they gathered their wits, the men from Bahía Kino would be coming after them. But they wanted to be prepared, for anything, just in case Sosa sent another party to check on the delay. At this moment, anything was possible.

The ride was long and hard, and Dutton couldn't work the horse team at the same speed as when they rode in to Bahía Kino. Their periodic rests were for the horses, not them. They could drink water or chew on beef jerky when they're riding, but the horses were continually at work and they needed time to cool down, drink a little water, and when the time was right, eat a little grain. Dutton always carried a small sack of grain in his saddle bag, never knowing when it might come in handy. Pang did take the time to stretch and work muscles that were sore from riding. Dutton could only watch him for a few seconds before he had to do the same thing. It was kind of like yawning, he thought, whenever someone else does it, you feel the need to do it too.

Dutton was putting the sack of grain back into the saddlebag when Pang came running down a slope of ground beside the road, pointing to the west. "They are coming."

Dutton peered in that direction. "How far away?"

"Not far. They are loping. We cannot outrun them."

Dutton put his hands on his hips and bit his bottom lip. "How many?"

"At least twenty. Two columns, all on horseback."

Dutton peered around in thought. "There's no way we can hide from them, either. We have only one choice."

"We could shoot their horses."

Dutton glanced at Pang, his brow furrowed and eyes wrinkled. "We ain't shootin' no damn horses."

"But you will shoot the men?"

"That's right, but not if I can help it."

"But you would agree that it would be better if they were on foot."

"That would definitely be an advantage."

"Then why not stop them . . . get them off of their horses? We will gain much if they are on foot."

Dutton smirked and leaned on his elbow against the wagon. "And how do you propose we do that?"

Pang raised a finger in the air and widened his eyes. "I have the perfect idea!"

Chapter Eleven

With Enrique's left shoulder in a bandage, and the muscle tissue extremely tender, he could not hold the bow and pull the string, but he could teach the boys, as he had promised. He took them to a place near the far end of an orange grove, where an adobe building stood and served as a perfect backdrop. The boys gathered bales of straw from the stable, brought them along and piled them against the wall. Enrique suggested a white cotton sack as a target, which had a somewhat faded printed image of a rooster on one side of the sack. "We will try to hit the *gallo,*" Enrique said.

They stood a good twelve meters from the target, and Felipe, the most eager, went first, while Javier sat on his knees, and Amado looked over Felipe's shoulder.

With Felipe as the example, Enrique showed them how to put the quiver criss-crossed on their backs so that they could easily reach over their right shoulder with the right hand and grab a new arrow after the shot. Then he showed them how to hold the weapon by having Felipe put his left hand firmly on the handle in the center of the bow, arm straight and extended toward the ground, and to nock the arrow with his right hand. The other two boys watched attentively as Enrique pointed above Felipe's hand to the top of the handle, which was made of small rope fibers wrapped around the handle several times.

"Here is where you rest the shaft of the arrow," Enrique said, helping him lay the arrow on the edge of the handle. Then he grabbed the back of the arrow and showed him the groove carved in the back tip. "And this we put on the bowstring, in a place where the arrow is pointed straight as you can get it, or at a very slight downward angle."

"Why at an angle?" Amado asked.

"That is a good question. Because you do not want the arrow to go up when you shoot it. That will really affect your accuracy. Straight is better, of course, but down is better than up. It takes practice to know the right place to put the back of the arrow, but here I have put some pigment from a red berry on the string, so that you know where to put it."

Enrique then demonstrated how to keep the left arm straight, and once the arrow was nocked properly, he had Felipe raise his left hand up, keeping his arm extended straight in front of him. Without holding the bow, he had the boys look at him as he simulated the arm positions. "When you pull the bowstring back, the end of the arrow should be between the index and middle knuckles." He reached down and wrapped those two fingers around the bowstring. "Like so."

Felipe followed his instructions and the arrow was properly nocked.

Once the arrow was secure on the handle, Enrique simulated the draw, by keeping his left arm extended straight out in front of him, and pulling his right hand back just below the eye.

"When your right hand his here, you can look straight down the arrow at your target." He glanced at each of the boys. *"Entiendes?"*

"Si," they all said simultaneously.

"Okay," Enrique said, nodding toward the cloth sack. "Find your target and see if you can hit the *gallo.*"

Felipe studied the cloth sack then looked back at Enrique nervously. "Now?"

"*Si,* try it."

The boy did as Enrique said, and his arm shook from the tension as he pulled back on the string. He let off without shooting. "It is very tight."

"Si," Enrique said, flexing his arm. "You will need to work on building strength in your arms. But you will eventually get used to it. Go on. Try it."

Felipe instinctively took a deep breath then aimed forward, pulled back the string with all of his might, as far back as he could, his arms shaking, then he let go. The arrow whiffled and thudded on the ground below the target, creating a small cloud of dust. The other boys laughed and Felipe lowered his head in embarrassment.

Enrique scolded them. "Do not laugh. You will be next, and you may not do as well. Then who will be laughing?" Enrique immediately turned back to Felipe. "Do not be discouraged. This was only your first try. It takes much practice to become a good hunter with a bow and arrow."

"But I aimed right at the *gallo,*" Felipe said. "Just as you told me to do."

"No, I told you to find your *target.* Your target is not always what you want to hit, because there are other things to consider."

"What do you mean?"

"Well, for example, the distance from the

target. You are about twelve meters from the *gallo,* and it is possible that you need to aim higher, because the arrow will drop in flight. Since you hit the ground, it is conceivable that you need to aim at a spot above the *gallo,* and *that* is your target. But pick a spot, and don't forget it, because if it is wrong, you will need to know where to adjust. *Entiendes?*"

Felipe nodded. "But how will I know where the target is?"

"That is a very good question, and it can only be answered with experience and much practice. I have been shooting the bow and arrow since I was a boy." Enrique smiled at Javier. "Much younger than Javier, even. All those years until now I have gained much practice. I know distance, I know wind, and I know my own strength for pulling the bowstring, which can change as I get older and stronger. All of these things build knowledge and accuracy. But it all comes with much practice."

"So if we practice, we can be as good as you someday?" Felipe said.

Enrique smiled. "*Si, mi hijo,* maybe even better."

Felipe smiled and then made his target. He reached behind his shoulder and grabbed a new arrow, went through all of the proper motions, and though shaky, he pulled back the bowstring as far as he could, then released, and the arrow hit the straw bale six inches from the cloth sack. Felipe's eyes rounded.

"Very good," Enrique said. "You made a good adjustment. The height is perfect. Now you just need to move a bit to the left. Did you remember where you aimed before?"

"Si," Felipe said.

"Very good. Then make another adjustment and try again."

Felipe studied the area and found his new target, and once again extended the bow outward, pulled back on the bowstring, peered down the arrow, then released, and the arrow made a perfect thud into the cloth sack right in the middle of the rooster.

The boy smiled widely.

Enrique put an arm around him "Very good!"

Amado rubbed Felipe's hair. "You did it *hermano*!"

"Okay," Enrique said. "Who is next?"

Amado stepped forward. "I am next." He took the quiver from Felipe, hung it around his arm, and then grabbed the bow.

"Okay," Enrique said. "Remember . . . find your target, and practice."

Amado looked at the cotton sack, lifted

the bow and extended his left arm. "Only I will not be shooting *gallos.* I am going to kill Sosa."

Enrique put a hand on Amado's wrist and pushed the bow downward. The two of them made eye contact and Enrique could see the anger in his eyes.

"Do not have hate in your heart, Amado. If that is all you want, then I will not teach you. Only learn these things for good, not evil."

"Sosa deserves to die."

"That is not for you to decide. Yes, he has done bad things to many people, but his life and death are in the hands of God, not us. It is only right for us to defend ourselves, and protect those we love, but not to be the aggressors. *Entiendes.*"

Amado shook his head. "No, I do not understand."

"Why, Amado?"

"Because I have heard the legend. The Demon Warrior killed your family, and you went after him. It was for revenge . . . for blood. And you found him, and you killed him."

"That is only partly true, *mi hijo.* I was very young when the Demon Warrior killed my family. I was raised by a priest, who taught me many things, and one of them was not to act out of vengeance, and to be patient. I was a grown man when I went after Valdar, and it was only because he had stolen women . . . family of my friend Pang Lo. When Pang came to me, I knew it was my destiny to help him . . . to help him rescue his family. That was an act of good."

Amado absorbed all that Enrique told him, but he did not seem convinced. "But you got to kill the Demon Warrior. There is justice in that."

"No, I did not kill him. It was someone else in our group. But I soon learned that it does not matter who does it, what matters is that justice is served. Right?"

Amado looked to the ground and nodded. *"Si."* He looked back up at Enrique. "When you were a boy, you did not want to kill the Demon Warrior?"

"I did, Amado. Just as you want to kill Sosa. But if not for the priest, I would not have learned how bad it was for my heart."

Amado looked soberly into Enrique's eyes. "You are like the priest now."

Enrique smiled and gently put his hand on the back of the boy's neck. "*Si, mi hijo.* The priest taught me many good things."

Sosa slammed a fist on the table. His eyes were wide and fierce. "Find her now!"

"We are looking, *patrón,*" Chavón said. "We have asked everywhere, and no one knows anything. Except the girls downstairs, who saw her leave out the back door. That is all."

Sosa stepped closer to Chavón and extended his anger with clenched teeth and a steady look into his eyes. "Why do you insult me, Chavón? Do not tell me no one knows. Somebody knows something! And you turn this town upside down until you find her!"

"Si, patrón."

Sosa kept glaring. "And what is happening with Fernando Jiménez?"

"We are still working on it, *patrón.*"

"Working on it? I did not tell you to work on it, I told you to DO IT!"

"Si, patrón."

Though faint and somewhat muffled, Fernando had heard the gunshots which broke the monotony of an already restless night. He sat up in his bed and lit a lantern, then poured himself a glass of water. He carried the cup and paced the floor of the small, musty room, and stopped when he heard a knock on the door. It was early for breakfast, he thought. And why are they knocking?

"Who is there?"

"Breakfast." It was a female voice.

Fernando hesitated a moment, but finally answered. "You need permission to enter?"

Keys jingled and the door finally opened and after the guard backed away, there stood Guadalupe carrying a large tray with two covered plates, a steaming mug of coffee, and a clear glass of *jugo de mandarina.*

The two of them stared at each other in silence and then Guadalupe walked into the room. "*Hola,* Fernando."

"Lupe?"

Guadalupe walked past him and set the tray on the table. She turned and looked soberly at him. "Eat, before it gets cold."

Fernando stepped slowly toward her and suddenly they fell into each other's arms and Guadalupe wept.

"Mi amor," Fernando said. *"Mi dulce, amor."*

Fernando leaned back. "Why are you here?"

Guadalupe let go and turned away. "I left. It took many years to find the courage, but I finally left." She reached over to the tray and removed the two covers from the plates. One was filled with hot corn tortillas, the other with ham and black beans.

Fernando stepped up behind her, his chin over her shoulder. "But Sosa will kill you."

She looked up and then reached down to

her side and held his hand. "I would rather die then stay there another day." Then she turned to face him, putting both of her hands on his chest, and then looked up into his eyes. "When I heard that you were caught as a spy, and would not go back to Sosa, I knew it was now or never."

Fernando nodded. "Those gunshots I heard. Were they for me or you?"

Guadalupe shrugged, and then turned back toward the tray. "Maybe they were for both of us."

"What are you going to do now?"

"Fernando, you should sit down and eat."

He turned her around and grabbed both of her hands. "Lupe, this could be a new beginning for us. Let's get out of here. Go somewhere far away."

"*Si,* I would love that. But not until after it is over."

"Until what is over?"

"Sosa is planning a raid on the *hacienda.* Constanza, and *El Trio,* they are preparing for it."

He let go of her hands and grabbed her shoulders firmly. "But that is too dangerous for you!"

She looked at him angrily then jerked away from his grasp. "My entire life has been spent on the edge of hell. So what is danger now? No, you will stay down here until it is over. And then, I will come and get you."

"But Lupe, what if you don't?"

She paused and looked at him tenderly. "Then you will know our destiny."

Dutton got down on his knees, leaned over and peered inside the narrow, rocky crevasse, and then he heard them. He rose back up wide-eyed, looking at Pang. "Rattlesnakes?"

"Yes," Pang smiled. "A whole den of them. Horses are terrified of rattlesnakes!"

"Yeah, well . . . so am I."

"But it is perfect!"

"How the hell is it perfect?"

"We create a diversion."

"A diversion? These people down here are used to rattlesnakes. They know how to handle them."

Pang put a hand on Dutton's shoulder. "Help me. You will see."

Dutton peered back inside the dark crevasse, heard the rattles again then swallowed. "Help you? No, God help *me*."

Vázquez rode in the lead with Hilario beside him and leading the other column, the men on their horses ahead of the wagon teams that followed at the end. The lieutenant, now prisoner, rode contently with a slight grin on his face the entire time, but the colonel paid him no mind, keeping his eyes on the road ahead, and on the wagon tracks below.

Eventually the colonel saw something ahead that caused him to squint, lean a little forward in the saddle, and then lean a bit to the side so he could see around his horse's head. The closer he rode, the more perplexed he became. It looked to be bunches of dry desert grasses and twigs from the thornscrub, but the piles were evenly placed across the roadway, and he counted six of them. Vázquez was experienced enough with surprises that he knew to expect anything, which caused him to rise up and look around for other obscure signs of potential trouble.

The area around them was mostly flat, with occasional washes, slopes into shallow gulches, but the colonel had seen trouble come from just about anywhere. When he got within two horse lengths of the scrub piles, he held up his hand and stopped the party. Before dismounting he looked down at the wagon tracks and saw that they continued on, even beyond the scrub piles, as far as he could see. He glanced over to a smirking Hilario.

"A bit odd, don't you think colonel?" Hilario said.

Vázquez ignored him and dismounted. He looked back to his men and held up a hand. "All of you stay where you are, but be on full alert."

The colonel led his horse by the reins following the wagon tracks, and when he got to the first scrub pile, he pushed it aside with his boot, revealing a coiling, startled rattlesnake in a shallow hand-dug pit. His horse whinnied and stepped backward but Vázquez kept a hold of the reins.

Hilario burst out in laughter. "Ah, colonel. Did your friends leave you a little surprise?"

Vázquez looked all around him for other signs, and since he saw none he shouted back to his men. "Everyone dismount but keep your horses away from this area, and keep a good hold on them." He pointed to another one of his men. "You, come and help me. Have someone else hold your horse."

The man did as the colonel ordered, and after they swiped away the other small piles of scrub, it revealed exactly what Vázquez thought it would: five more rattlesnakes. The soldier helped the colonel lift the snakes out of the small holes using the barrel tip of his rifle, and he carried each one of the angry serpents far off the side of the road and dropped them into the wash.

When they were finished, the soldier walked up to the Vázquez. "That is all of them, colonel."

Vázquez kept looking around the area. "I'm not so sure about that."

"Why, colonel?"

"It was definitely an attempt to slow us down, but taking the time to do this would slow them down too. No, I don't think this is over."

Before he could find another clue he saw something fly through the air and quickly realized it was another snake. The snake landed amongst the crowd of men and their horses, which no doubt caused a scurry. The men tried to hold on to their horses, but then another snake, and another, fell to the ground and before the colonel could locate where they were coming from, twenty horses had reared and broke free from the men. Even the men found themselves falling and scrambling to get away from the snakes, and the horses that were attached to the wagons were difficult for the drivers to handle. Before Vázquez thought it could get any worse, gunshots rang out, with bullets hitting the ground near the front of the horse teams, and the already spooked animals lunged and took off in a gallop forcing the wagon drivers to fall backward or off to the side into the ground. Two of the wagons pulling the guns sped off into the gulches, crashing and tearing apart, wagon wheels breaking from their axels and rolling away in the dust. The other wagon, which carried the dead, sped off down the road, past Vázquez, with the driver unable to stop it.

Vázquez drew his pistol and located where the shots were coming from, and while holding on to his horse's reins with the other hand, he fired into the gulch, but it was no use. The shooter had stopped, and the damage was already done. All of the horses and riders were separated, and the frightened animals ran hard in all directions.

Vázquez holstered his pistol, then took off his hat and threw it hard to the ground. "Dammit!"

He looked up at Hilario, who had managed to keep his horse from getting into the fray, and sat there laughing. "Ah, colonel. What a great job you are doing leading these men. If you keep up the good work, you might have them home in time for the *fiesta*!"

Vázquez had had enough, and he dropped

the reins to his horse and marched over to Hilario, grabbed him by the arm and jerked him out of the saddle to a hard, dusty landing in the road.

"Get up!" Vázquez said.

Hilario rose to his elbows, his face half covered with dust, and he looked up at the colonel with his familiar arrogant gaze. "You are finished. Do with me what you want, but you have failed. And Sosa has only one way to reward failure."

Vázquez stood there, arms hanging at his sides, fists clenched, breathing hard, glaring down at the lieutenant. As much as he hated to hear it, Hilario was right, which meant that he had nothing more to lose than he already had, and that his next move would be no more condemning. He removed the pistol from his holster, pointed it at Hilario and cocked the hammer.

Hilario laughed. "Kill me and you have no chance. Untie me and I will help you. I can explain things to Sosa, and I know how to gain redemption from him."

"Redemption?" Vázquez said. "Lieutenant, the only redemption you are going to need now is from God."

Hilario's haughty grin quickly changed to a frightful sneer as the colonel locked his arm tight and pulled the trigger. The shot in the heart put Hilario flat on his back, and his eyes squinting shut. Vázquez looked up at the frenzy around him, men chasing after their horses, and realized for the first time in his life that he had been walking the wrong path. There was no future for him working with or for men like Hilario or Sosa. Who were the men that did all of this? Who was this *El Trio*? He also knew that there was no future for him as a deserter, or for any of these men that followed him. No, he needed a new plan, and this time he would look after no one but himself, live or die, all in the eyes of the mighty Creator.

Chapter Twelve

They rode into the *hacienda* in the middle of the night. Sereno was the first to see them, and he woke the stable worker, who lit a lantern then opened the double doors and Dutton drove the wagon inside. Pang rode in behind and after he dismounted he greeted Sereno with a smile and a pat on the shoulder.

Dutton crawled off of the wagon seat, squatted and grimaced from his aching legs and hips. The stable worker was quick to take the harnesses off the horses and lead them to stalls, and then he tended to Pang's and Dutton's horses.

The three men walked outside and closed the double doors behind them, with Sereno carrying a lantern. When they walked into the courtyard and headed toward the main *casa,* Dutton stopped and looked around, then pointed. "Over there."

Pang and Sereno looked to where he was

pointing. Though it was dark, the lantern lights that hung throughout the *hacienda* cast just enough light that they could see all of the vantage points.

"It's in the open," Dutton said, "and you can see down the lane that leads to the road. And if need be, we can rotate toward the fields or into the courtyard."

Pang nodded. "I agree, it looks like the perfect place."

"I don't know about perfect," Dutton said, "but it's the best idea I have unless something better comes up."

"When do we tell Señora Ramírez?" Pang asked.

Dutton looked up at the star filled sky. "We have a few more hours until daylight. Let's get some sleep, and then bring the *señora* to the stable to see it for herself, then we can make our plans."

The sun had not yet made its presence over the east adobe wall as Enrique leaned against the side of the *casa,* drinking a hot cup of coffee and looking out over the wall at the blending coral and blue of the sunrise. He rolled his shoulder from the tenderness of the healing wound, and thought about the doctor's encouragement, that after a week of healing, to use his bow to help rebuild the strength in his arm. The doctor said it would take some time, but each day to try and pull a little farther on the string. As it was, Enrique could barely hold the bow and extend his arm out straight with out a powerful, piercing pain, but the doctor said that was normal, and that the nerves around the muscle would need time to heal.

Before he could think much more about it, a shuffle of feet caught his attention and he looked around to find Emanuela walking toward him. They greeted each other with smiles, and she clutched her shawl tighter around her neck as she stood beside him and gazed over the wall at the colors of the sunrise.

"It is a beautiful morning," she said.

Enrique followed her gaze. "Yes, it is."

She looked up at him. "The boys cannot stop talking about what you have taught them . . . about shooting the bow and arrow."

"I am glad to do it."

"It is good that they have found someone else to look up to. I cannot tell you how much it calms my heart."

"I must be careful, though, to make sure they do not take my teachings the wrong way. They must use that knowledge only for good."

"You are a good teacher. I am sure they will."

"I hope you are right."

"This morning they were up very early, off into the wilderness looking for trees to make their own bows and arrows."

Enrique laughed. "That is good. That should keep them busy for a while."

"Yes, it should."

At that moment Jose walked up behind them and they turned to acknowledge him.

"Señor," Jose said. "Dutton and Pang, they made it back."

Enrique shared a smile with Emanuela, and then turned back to Jose. "That is great news! Where are they?"

"They are about to meet for breakfast with Señora Ramírez, but before they do, they are meeting in the stable. They asked for you to join them."

They met with cheerful greetings, and along with Dutton and Pang, Constanza Ramírez was there for the private gathering. Enrique walked around to the back of the wagon. "So this is it?"

Dutton and the others followed him. Constanza rested her hands on her hips. "It is amazing enough that you made it back, but to have brought this back with you?"

"It wasn't easy, ma'am," Dutton said.

"There were three of them. Since we could only bring one, we did all we could to keep them from using the others. Though it's not likely they will ever use them against us, it's still possible." He rested a hand on the end of the gun barrels. "But if they do, we at least have a fighting chance."

Constanza did not look all too relieved. "It looks so deadly, and destructive."

Dutton nodded. "It is ma'am. If we have any idea when Sosa might make his move, I would suggest getting all of the women and children to safety. When bullets start flying from this thing, it's like a hail storm. What we need is a real good plan for when it happens."

"Si," Constanza said. "All of you, come to breakfast, and we will talk about this plan."

Dutton rested a hand on Pang's shoulder. "A hot meal sure sounds a lot better than jerky, eh *compadre*?"

Pang put a finger on his chin and looked upward. "Hmm, I was thinking that rattlesnake stew sounded very appetizing."

Dutton grunted and shook his head. "Well, you have at it, pardner."

Sosa and Chavón were led out into the courtyard behind the headquarters, where eight of his men stood, dirty and weary, next to a wagon that carried three dead bodies and a dozen empty ammunition boxes. They were all silent as he looked them over, and took particular notice of the solider with a wounded leg.

"I do not see Lieutenant Hilario," Sosa said.

The wounded solider looked around nervously. "He is in the wagon, *patrón.*"

Chavón walked over to the back of the wagon and lifted the canvas to reveal the three dead men; Hilario lying on top, his head tilted sideways, his eyelids half open. Chavón looked up at Sosa and nodded.

Sosa walked over to the back of the wagon and looked in as Chavón continued to hold up the tarp. He looked at each of the faces of the dead, then saw Hilario's hands sticking up, tied at the wrists. "Why are his hands tied?"

The wounded soldier kept acting as the spokesman. "Colonel Vázquez, *patrón.* Lieutenant Hilario, he tried to keep the gold for himself instead of giving it to the smugglers for the guns. The colonel did not approve, so he arrested the lieutenant."

"Colonel Vázquez?"

"Si, patrón."

Sosa stepped away from the wagon and looked directly at the wounded soldier.

"Then why is the lieutenant dead?"

"The colonel shot him, *patrón.* After the attack."

"Attack?"

"Si, patrón. About halfway here. It was *El Trio."*

Sosa's face hardened. *"El Trio."*

"Si, patrón."

"And where is the colonel now?"

"He ordered us to come here, and he ordered his men to stay with the guns."

"My guns?"

"Si, patrón."

"So the colonel sent you back here, and he stayed with the guns?"

"No, *patrón."*

"No?"

"We do not know where he went. He left."

"He left."

"Si," the wounded soldier looked around nervously. "With the gold."

Sosa stared at the soldier, his face almost ashen from holding his breath, then he turned and looked back at Chavón. "Organize a detachment of twenty men. We are going after my guns."

The wounded soldier took a step closer to Sosa. *"Patrón?"*

"What is it?"

"I feel I must tell you, that you are going

to need wagons for the guns. The wagons were destroyed in the attack. The guns were damaged, and the ammunition, it is gone."

Chavón narrowed his eyes and walked quickly around the wagon and reached over and opened one of the ammunition boxes. He lifted it out of the wagon and held it open for Sosa to see.

Sosa looked blank faced at the empty box and then turned back to the wounded soldier. He looked him up and down. "What is your name?"

"Raul Gonzalez, *patrón.*"

"Raul." Sosa studied him. "Go inside and see my personal doctor." Sosa pointed at the soldier's thigh. "Have him clean that up, and do whatever is necessary to get you back in shape. And get a new uniform. When I am back, we will have a ceremony, and you will be promoted to lieutenant."

Raul smiled slightly, and then saluted Sosa. *"Si, patrón!"*

Sosa turned back to Chavón. "You heard him, get the wagons, too. And when we return, we are going to take *El Trio* through the gates of hell."

It was rare for Sosa to go very far outside Hermosillo, but the gun shipment was too important to all that he had planned for his future. Besides, it seemed now that whenever he sent a special squad out to do something, they failed, and all because of three men who seemed to have incredible luck. And that's what he believed it was. No three men could be that powerful or cunning to defeat all of Sosa's well-trained and organized militia. No, something else was happening inside his army. There was a breakdown in competency, and he was going to get to the bottom of it immediately.

When they arrived at the scene of the attack, a camp was set up, and the men had tried to repair the wagons, but to no avail. Sosa ordered them all to hook up the guns to the new wagons, and to tear down camp and prepare to return to Hermosillo. The men from Bahía Kino were ordered to go with the number two and three men of his elite force, west to the port city to look for Colonel Vázquez. That was where the wounded solider, Raul Gonzalez, said he was going.

The young man, soon to be promoted to lieutenant, also mentioned his suggestion to take the guns to the gunsmith in Hermosillo to be repaired, and that a man of such expertise would likely have a solution to the problem with the ammunition and the missing magazine clips. Sosa was impressed with this man's ability to think, and confirmed his belief that no one was indispensible. Somewhere in the ranks were men with capabilities that could easily take the place of those who were gone.

When they returned to Hermosillo, that is where they took the guns, directly to Ortiz Molina on the south side of town, a former sergeant in the Mexican army, who as a young man had served under Benito Juarez when he overthrew Santa Anna. He was an expert in arms, and though he had come back to Hermosillo to be with his family, he found great pleasure working with the *policía* and repairing their guns. Sosa had heard of him, had sent repairs to him, but had never paid him a personal visit. This, he thought, was the perfect opportunity to meet the man with such skills.

Ortiz was standing over a red hot piece of steel, that he held with long metal tongs and bending it with a hammer, when Sosa and his men rode up in front of his gunsmith shop with the wagons. The gray-headed gunsmith set everything down and walked out into the daylight to get a better look at what he thought he saw, and he was right, they were Gatling guns. He paid very little attention to the men who brought them, but instead reached over the sides of the wagon and inspected every little detail of the weapon. Then he looked back to the other wagon, and saw that there were two.

After Sosa had dismounted, Chavón and his men followed suit and he walked up to Ortiz. Sosa removed the glove from his hand and extended it forward.

Ortiz looked at his hand, and then looked up at Sosa. "My hands are very dirty from work."

Sosa raised his eyebrows and shrugged. "Very well." He removed his other glove then nodded toward the closest Gatling gun. "These guns, as you can see, have had, well . . . let us say, an accident. I am sure that Santa Anna and Juarez never had as much trouble. Even they would have had limbers for their cannons. But I have to have them attached to wagons by doubletrees." He shook his head then studied Ortiz. "I have heard many great things about your work. I am told that you are the man who can get them in perfect working order."

Ortiz took another glance at the guns. "These guns can kill many people very quickly."

Sosa grunted a short laugh. "Yes, that is what I am told."

"What is wrong with them?"

Sosa nodded and pointed and walked him closer to the guns. "The chambers inside have come in contact with sand and mud. They need taken apart, cleaned, and reassembled. Can you do that?"

Ortiz looked over the back of the guns very closely. He peered down inside the breech chambers, then underneath at the ejector openings. He grabbed the crank handles and tried to turn them. He looked back down at Sosa and nodded. "*Sí.* It will take much work, but I can do it."

"*Muy bien.* And one other thing, the ammunition for these guns has, well . . . it has disappeared. I am told you might be able to help us find replacements?"

Ortiz stepped around the gun to the front and stuck his pinky finger inside the opening of one of the barrels. He nodded again. "*Sí,* I can come up with something."

"Excelente," Sosa said. "When could I expect all of this ready? You see, I need it for a special occasion on Constitution Day."

Ortiz looked at Sosa a moment, then nervously at all of the men. "*Sí,* I can have it all ready the night before."

Sosa smiled. "*Muy bien!* Our newly decorated lieutenant was right. You were the perfect man for this job. I will send men with wagons over here to get the guns the night before." Sosa turned to the men with him and clapped his hands. "Quickly, help wheel these guns into Señor Molina's shop. He has much work to do."

Ortiz stood aside as the men worked quickly and unhooked the tongues from the makeshift pintles on the doubletree, and rolled them inside the gunsmith's shop. He pointed to an area where they left them, and then he watched them all walk back out to their horses. After a grinning nod from Sosa, accompanied by a tip of his hat, they all followed their *patrón* down the busy street and out of sight.

Though matters seemed somewhat back to normal at the *hacienda,* everyone knew that a great storm loomed on the horizon. Pang continued with his daily lessons in breathing and self-defense, and Dutton worked with them on how to load and shoot their firearms. All of this was done with small groups and in hourly shifts, where they'd work in the fields, then come in for their lesson, then back out to the fields. This way, Constanza said, no one would notice anything out of the ordinary.

Enrique continued to work with the boys and their archery lessons, and he also spent part of the afternoon helping them build their own bows and arrows with the materials they found in the wilderness. He was impressed by their finding of willow branches, which were very flexible and good for the bows. They also found a dead pine tree in the foothills, and its branches were perfectly round and naturally hardened, which would serve well for arrows.

Since he knew that finding indigenous arrowheads would be very difficult, he showed them how to carefully carve sharp points onto the tip of the arrow. "These tips can be just as deadly to any animal you are hunting."

After Amado had finished his bow, he was eager to try it on their cloth sack marker. They all gathered around, and after a few shots, Amado was hitting the target proficiently. Following a celebration of a perfect shot into the printed *gallo,* the boys looked behind them to see that they had an audience.

Enrique turned to see Guadalupe standing a few meters away. He smiled at her. "Ah, *señora,* we are just practicing."

Guadalupe took a few steps closer. "I see that. And doing very well, too."

Amado held up his bow. "Would you like to try it, *señora*?"

"Oh . . . no, *gracias.* I will just watch you."

Amado nocked another arrow, then drew back and took careful aim. After he released, the arrow stuck perfectly into the center of the *gallo.*

Everyone applauded.

"Bravo," Guadalupe said. *"Muy bien."*

Enrique turned to the other boys. "You all keep practicing. I am going to visit with Señora Rojas."

The boys did as Enrique said and he walked back to where Guadalupe stood watching.

"You are doing a good job with these boys," she said.

"I am enjoying it. It reminds me so much of my youth. They need good direction. Plus, it gives me something to do while I am healing."

"Your shoulder," she said. "It is okay?"

"Yes, it is fine. Still very tender, but the doctor is confident I will heal."

"That is good."

They both kept watching the boys, and after Felipe made a perfect shot into the *gallo,* they all applauded.

"He reminds me so much of my son," Guadalupe said.

"You have a son?"

"Well," she said, looking solemnly at her feet. "I did once. He died."

"I am sorry, *señora.* I know how that feels."

"This life . . . it is hard, no?"

Enrique nodded. "Yes, it is. But I have found much good in it also."

"Unfortunately I have not. Many years ago I cried until no more tears came out. I feel I have already cried enough for a lifetime. All there is now is bitterness."

"You are free from all of that now, *señora.* What you need is more time. Time around good people. Time to heal."

"Si," she said, watching Felipe nock an arrow. "I suppose you are right."

Ortiz Molina had done business with many of Sosa's men. Most of them brought him guns with jamming problems, or they had problems with sighting, but most of them seemed harmless and were friendly, and the gunsmith had no issues with them. But occasionally he would hear them talk about Sosa, the people he had killed, or the things they were planning, and it all reminded him of the days he fought with Benito Juarez, and how they fought to bring down the tyrannical reign of Antonio López de Santa Anna. The stories were troubling to his mind, and he tried his best to ignore them, but there were many great people who lived in fear of Sosa, and Ortiz knew, from history, it would never end unless Sosa ended. But he was too old now to fight, and too worn out to try. What little physical ability he had left was in his fingers, for the smallest of details, but he still had his mind, and the best he could tell it was all still there.

It was only two days before Sosa showed up with the Gatling guns, when two officers came to him to have their rifles sighted, and he overheard them talking about the upcoming raid on the *Hacienda de Ramírez.* Though he didn't know the Ramírez family personally, he knew enough about the operation and the people who worked there to know that they were honest and hard-working, and that Sosa's plan of attack was nothing more than evil and tyrannical, just like what he'd experienced with Santa Anna. Not once did Ortiz think of getting involved, or trying to stop it, until the moment when Sosa and his men rode up with the wagons and the Gatling guns. Though it was almost haunting to see them, he feared having to live with the guilt of knowing that he helped the oppressor. It was a horrible feeling, to be in such a position. A position where he had to make sure the guns worked or he would be killed. And if they worked perfectly, then he would contribute to evil and have to live with that knowledge the rest of his life. It was the most troubling circumstance he'd ever faced, and though he was too old to take sides and join the fight, he had to find a way to help the meek, without the king's army knowing.

As he took apart the Gatling guns, it was easy to tell that someone was trying to stop Sosa from using them. They did a fairly good job of it — the sand and mud were clear antagonists to moving metal parts, but as Sosa quickly figured out, all they had to do was be cleaned, and then put back together.

Ortiz stood there, looking over the many disassembled parts, wondering how he could make the gun function, but not make it successful. This was not like a rifle, where one could adjust the sight for accuracy. The general idea of the gun was to shoot a lot of bullets quickly, to spray them like a swarm of deadly hornets. Since the magazines were missing, he could easily replace their function with a metal tray that attached to the breech opening, which would allow the ammunition to drop in using the laws of gravity. But then was the question of ammunition. He looked over to the many empty, wooden ammunition boxes on the floor, and then to his own supply. The weapons, they were old Gatling guns, that used .50-caliber cartridges, the same as the carbines from those days. Ortiz had shot thousands of those rounds in his time, and he walked over to his own store of wooden boxes, scores of them filled with a more modern brass shell casing with a removable primer. He held one of the empty casings in front of him and studied it carefully. Yes, it would work. It would take most of the night to get the guns cleaned and put back together, and many hours of punching out old primer caps, adding new ones, and loading with the proper ammunition. Yes, it would work. He had exactly what Sosa needed.

Promotion ceremonies were rarely a planned event, and more often than not, they were spontaneous. When someone was killed and to be replaced, or someone was recognized for a special skill, then it needed doing and Sosa made it happen. He had a stage constructed near the headquarters for just such a ceremony. Members of his *policía* had formed a brass band with a solitary drummer, and they were called upon for music during every ceremony.

The top five in Sosa's elite squad joined him on the stage, in order by their ranking number. In front of the stage were rows of wooden chairs, the colonels in the front row, then the lieutenants, and all other soldiers stood behind them. When the brass band was done playing, Sosa stood and acknowledged the widow of Colonel Rodríguez, dressed in all black, and he gave her a shiny medal in honor of her late husband's service. She left the stage weeping, and then Raul Gonzalez, his face clean shaved, now dressed in a crisp uniform, but still limping, walked up and stood to attention, delivering a prideful salute.

Sosa pinned a special medal for bravery onto his tunic, and then his lieutenant stripes. After another salute, he pointed to the chairs below, where he was to join the other ranking officers. They all applauded as he walked off the stage, and Sosa turned toward the band and nodded. They played a celebratory tune of their own making, and after Sosa sat down, the main gates opened and in rode two guards on horses, followed by a guard driving the prisoner wagon.

All heads turned to acknowledge who was in the wagon, as this was a very surprising moment for the entire regime. Very few knew who Sosa had sentenced to death. Even though they might know who had it coming, it was quite often that the condemned couldn't be found. They were not surprised, however, to see the two men of Sosa's elite squad, only known to him as number nineteen and number twenty-six, still in dark clothing, charcoal on their faces mixed with blood from their brutish capture. But they were surprised to see a colonel, the one they rarely got to see, from Bahía Kino, Colonel Vázquez. The skin around one of his eyes was black and blue, the eyelid half swollen shut. Blood dripped from a cut on his cheek and from one on his lip.

The guards dismounted and walked to the back of the prisoner wagon and opened the gate. They dragged all three men, fettered by their hands and ankles, and took them to a place along the adobe wall. A priest in a brown robe appeared and walked along reciting scripture in Latin to each of them.

Sosa left the stage and walked along in front of the doomed men, and one of the guards followed closely. He stopped in front of each one and looked them in the eyes. "Do you understand your failure and your sentence?"

The man he only knew as number twenty-six nodded. *"Si, patrón."*

The guard followed up by placing a blindfold around the man's eyes, and did the same to the next one after Sosa's final words. Then Sosa stopped in front of Colonel Vázquez, whose pitiful, mournful gaze did nothing to alter Sosa's final inquiry.

"I don't suppose you have had a change of heart?"

The colonel did not answer, nor look him in the eye.

"Very well," Sosa said. "Do you understand your failure, and your sentence?"

This time the colonel's one good eye shifted and looked directly at Sosa. He spat a bloody wad of saliva at Sosa's feet, and then looked back up in disgust. "You will not know this today, but very soon you will know that I did not fail."

Sosa glared at him for a moment, then turned and nodded at the guard. The guard blindfolded him and stepped away. The air around them was very still until Sosa nodded to the drummer, who began his rapid beat, and the firing squad marched in unison into the open area. They stopped ten meters in front of the men and stood at attention.

Sosa nodded at the drummer, who stopped, and then he yelled out to the firing squad. "Ready!"

The squad stood sideways and raised the weapons to their chests.

"Aim!"

The guns were raised and pointed directly at the doomed men. Though most of the people there had witnessed these types of executions before, the feeling of anxiety was never absent.

"Fire!"

The blasts from the rifles sent the men flying backward into the wall, and though the two former elite soldiers immediately fell onto the ground, Vázquez was slow to drop, grimacing as he started to slide downward. All eyes were on him, and just as the firing squad was about to shoot him again, he lifted his chin, and regardless of what little air his lungs had left, he cried out loud enough for all of Hermosillo to hear. *"Viva El Trio!"*

CHAPTER THIRTEEN

Several of the soldiers loaded the boxes of ammunition into the wagon, and before attaching the tongues of the Gatling guns to the doubletree, Sosa ordered Lieutenant Gonzales to push both of them out into the street and test them. Gonzales instructed four soldiers to wheel the guns out and point them toward the side of the building. Just as he was about to retreat to grab a box of ammunition, he nearly ran into Ortiz, who was standing there between him and the wagon, extending out his hands, cupped together and holding several shiny brass cartridges.

Gonzalez nodded and took the cartridges from Ortiz and carried them to the guns, dropping them one-by-one into each of the newly designed metal feeders. When he was finished, he turned and nodded to Sosa.

"Very well," Sosa said. "Now we just need something to shoot at."

Gonzalez looked nervously at Sosa and then Sosa busted out laughing. Gonzalez was slow to follow, but eventually he laughed too, and at the same time he hurriedly located several clay pots of all sizes, many of them filled with water, and he had the soldiers help him line them up across the top of a table in front of the wall.

When he was finished he again nodded at Sosa, who pointed a hand back to him.

"Lieutenant Gonzalez," Sosa said. "Would you please assume the honor of testing these fine weapons and —" Sosa looked behind him at Ortiz. "— and the fine work of our gunsmith."

Gonzalez walked up behind one of the guns and grabbed the crank handle and turned it, which sent a spray of bullets into the arrangement of clay pots, causing them to shatter and water to splatter and spill onto the wall and table. It didn't take long for the few cartridges to be spent, and then Gonzalez walked to the other gun, which worked as fluidly as the first, annihilating what was left of the clay pots.

As the smoke from the guns was dissipating into the air, Sosa put his hands together, clapping and nodding at Gonzalez, and then turning to applaud the gunsmith. Ortiz nodded his thanks to Sosa, who walked up to him, once again extending a hand.

"Are your hands too dirty today, Señor Molina?"

Ortiz looked at his hand but accepted the shake.

Sosa gripped his hand firmly, looked at the gunsmith inquisitively and did not let go of his hand. "If all goes well in battle, there will be a medal in this for you. A medal of good service to your people."

Ortiz nodded. "*Gracias, señor.* Everything I do is for the better of my people."

Enrique did as the doctor instructed and used his bow as a tool to help rebuild his strength while the muscle tissue in his shoulder healed. He could be seen walking around the *hacienda* carrying his bow, occasionally stopping and extending his arms, grimacing from the pain as he tried to pull it all of the way. But the doctor insisted he work in small strides, pulling a little each time, with infrequent attempts to pull it farther.

He could also be seen with the boys, watching them practice with their own bows and arrows, instructing them on advanced techniques, and moving them farther away from their targets.

Emanuela was not sure that she approved

of these lessons, that it was too soon after their removal from Sosa's evil hand, and that their minds were still very impressionable and prone to violence. Enrique understood her concern, and assured her that every lesson came with many words of wisdom and morality, but no one can ever stop boys from being boys. This made her smile, and between those lessons, and his own rehabilitation, she encouraged him to walk with her and share his dreams.

"How long will you stay here, Enrique?" she asked.

"I do not know. I came here for a much different reason . . . to look for my grandfather, but now I have found myself in a situation that I cannot avoid. And, I cannot leave here knowing that this *hacienda* is unprotected."

She smiled. "I like you being here. I hope you will stay."

They stopped walking and he turned to face her, grabbing both of her hands and looking deep into her eyes. "I would love to stay, but I truly do not know the answer."

"Your answer, Enrique, and your reason, is looking into your eyes right now."

He nodded and rubbed his finger tips down her cheek. "I know, Emanuela. It is very difficult for me to know what to do.

This is the first time I have ever been in love."

She looked away shyly, then back up at him and closed her eyes and kissed him hard on the lips. When she backed away a single tear ran down her cheek. She continued to hold his hands while she looked up at him. "When you do know what you want, you will tell me, okay?"

He could see the hurt that was caused by his uncertainty, and before he could respond she let go of his hands and turned and walked away. He wanted to go after her, but something stopped him. A feeling, he knew, that was the same feeling that prompted the words he told her. It all boiled down to the question of his destiny, which he'd known since he was a boy that the answers often came to him unexpectedly, and with unequivocal direction.

Pang and Dutton spent a lot of time working with the people of the *hacienda,* and with Constanza, but especially her armed guards. They were the men most capable of using the new gun, if it was ever to be used, and they had to be trained. They all hoped that it would never come to that, but then they knew how serious Sosa was in his quest to own all of Sonora for himself, and, maybe someday, all of Mexico. Constanza was grateful for the help of *El Trio,* and now, more than ever, she felt there was hope in defeating Sosa.

Enrique and Sereno met with Pang and Dutton in the stable for their own special meeting. The question posed by Emanuela was also a good question for all of them.

Dutton was the first to respond. "I came here to help you fellers, and there was no time limit on it."

"But what about your family back in Missouri?" Enrique said.

"It's just my brother, and field hands are a penny a hundred up there. He'll fend just fine without me."

"I am here, too," Pang said. "For as long as it takes."

"But what about your trip back to China?" Enrique asked. "You have been planning that for a long time."

"I am sure that by the time that this is all over, they will still be building and sailing ships, and selling passage."

Enrique smiled, and then turned to Sereno. "And you are with us my friend?"

Sereno stepped forward, extending his hand, palm down. Enrique followed suit, putting his hand over Sereno's, and when the other two realized what they were doing, they joined the pact, and though the legend throughout the land was of three men, the legend of *El Trio,* the truth did not matter, in that together, then and now, were four men, with an unbreakable bond, a clear conscience, and an undeniable thirst for justice.

Chapter Fourteen

FEBRUARY 5, 1884, DÍA DE CONSTITUCIÓN

The day began early for the people of the *hacienda,* an hour before dawn, with a gathering at the chapel where Constanza Ramírez called upon everyone to join her in a morning of prayer. She was the first to walk forward and light a candle, bow to the Virgin Mary and make the cross over her chest. And they all followed, Jose, Emanuela, Guadalupe, Enrique, Pang, who did not make the cross, but only bowed his respects, and Dutton, who merely tipped his hat. The field workers crowded in — men, women, and children, and before long the entire chapel was decorated and illuminated by flickering candles.

They all prayed silently, and then in the haze of the early morning, went to their jobs, working in the fields as if it was just like any other day. Emanuela, however, with the assistance of Guadalupe and Constanza, gathered all of the children and the elderly, and took them inside the main *casa,* where they would stay until they knew for sure that it was over — that they either claimed victory over Sosa, or would have to surrender to his reign.

Amado led the major complaint from the three boys, that they were soldiers, trained to fight, and now knew how to use the bow and arrow, just like Enrique, but neither of them could win the argument over Constanza, who with her commanding voice put them into submission and down into the wine cellar, locked in their own room.

Pang walked with the workers to the orange groves, greeting and nodding at each of them, who began their duties of tilling the soil and pruning the orange trees. He stayed close to the palm-bordered lane that led to the *hacienda,* pacing the rows between the trees, and keeping a watchful eye on the main road.

Enrique walked through the cotton fields, stretching his arms and working his shoulder by pulling on the bowstring, but the only thing different today from other days was that his quiver was now on his back, filled with arrows. Like Pang, he also stayed close to the road, and at a distance where he could see anyone who might alert them to oncoming danger.

Dutton stayed back by the stable, preparing his horse to ride, and in close proximity of the guards, keeping and eye on the main opening to the *hacienda,* and anyone who might make an entrance. He also made sure his Winchester rifle and two Colt .45 revolvers were loaded and ready, as well as his gun belt filled with cartridges.

Sereno stayed close to the road, under the shade of a palm tree on the farthest corner of the cotton field, and the closest point to Hermosillo. He had been there most of the night, during the sunrise, and watched everyone leave the chapel and work their way into the fields. He could see Pang and Enrique, and he knew that they were also watching him.

The chill of the morning air was barely absorbed by the sun when Sereno saw the movement, and then heard the horse steps and rattles of the wagons. He stood straight and made sure of what was coming, and then he turned toward Enrique and whistled like a desert bird.

Enrique was the only one who understood that sound, and trusted it, and quickly turned to Pang and waved his whole arm to get his attention. Pang acknowledged him immediately, by returning the same wave, then looked back toward the main *casa,* stuck two fingers in his mouth and whistled at the guards.

The guards were quick to stand to attention, and they alerted their comrades, ten altogether, and then one of them ran to the stable. The anxious guard ran through the open door of the stable to a sliding stop. "*Señor,* they are here!"

Dutton thought for a moment then responded to the guard. "Okay, you know your positions."

"Si, señor."

The guard turned and ran back through the door into the courtyard and Dutton mounted his horse and trotted out into the opening. Before he went any farther, he stopped to look out toward the road. Sure enough, Sosa led his army of men, some on horseback, others on foot, and just as everyone had expected, hell was coming to breakfast.

Dutton turned his horse and loped out to the orange grove and found Pang. They both watched as Sosa and his *policía* marched down the road, and when the horse teams came into view, pulling the Gatling guns like cannons, they were equally astonished.

"They have the guns!" Pang said. "How is that possible?"

Dutton let out a long breath as he delivered his thousand-yard stare. "When it comes to war battles, anything is possible. We did what we could, and we got one of the guns out of the deal. We have to live with that."

"But that is two against one!"

"Just do what we do best, amigo, and if anything else, pray for a miracle."

"Ugh," Pang said. "I hate guns."

Dutton spurred his horse and rode around to check on the guards and make sure they were positioned as they had planned. He nodded toward the two guards that he'd trained on the Gatling gun. "It's time. Get it into position, and remember, wait until the proper range. That ammunition goes fast."

The two guards nodded and then ran to the stable where they opened the double doors and led out the horse team that was attached by harness to the tongue of the Gatling gun. Together the two men moved quickly to position the gun right at the end of the lane and to the entrance to the courtyard. They removed the doubletree from the tongue and then took the horses back to the stable to exchange them for another horse team attached to a wagon — a wagon that held all of the ammunition.

Sosa stopped at the other end of the lane on the road and ordered his colonels to get the men into position. All of the soldiers on foot ran the distance and spread out along the edge of the road at the ends of the fields. They stood ready as the men on horses scattered out behind them, and then the men leading the horse teams pulled the Gatling guns to where they pointed toward the field — one at each end, and the wagons of ammunition parked behind them.

Sosa sat on his horse with pride, next to Chavón, watching his *policía* work so fluidly. Suddenly he looked down the lane and extended a hand toward his number one man. "Hand me my field glasses."

Chavón produced the binoculars, and as Sosa peered through them, he inhaled deeply and then lowered the glasses into his lap.

"What is it *patrón*?" Chavón said.

He handed the binoculars back to him. "It appears we have located our missing gun."

Chavón lifted the glasses quickly to his eyes, looked for a few seconds, then lowered them. "Vázquez was right. It was *El Trio.*"

"Yes, well . . . it is all a game of chance,

and soon *El Trio* will be joining Colonel Vázquez in a game with the devil. We have a much better advantage. We are spread out, and we have more men. But, after a few rounds of hellfire from the Gatling guns, it will all be over very soon."

Sosa glanced out into the fields at the many workers, who now stood, staring at them. He looked down at each of the men with the Gatling guns, and all stood ready, waiting for his command. He took one last glance over the entire *hacienda,* and then raised his voice to all of the men. "Commence firing!"

Both Gatling guns rolled and fired, shrouded in their own smoke, and the many workers in the fields stood there, untouched, as were the orange trees, and the stalks of cotton. Dutton, Enrique, and Pang, who had fallen belly down to the ground, could not believe what they were seeing. Dutton jumped up, mounted his horse, and rode out quickly to the orange grove and yelled at the people to drop to the ground, but they remained standing, without fear, and without the will to cower.

Sosa rose up in his saddle and peered out into the fields. "What is happening?"

Lieutenant Gonzalez stood behind one of the guns as one soldier turned the crank handle and the other fed the cartridges, but he too was dumbfounded as to why there were no casualties, and as to how the many field workers merely stood there like ghosts, unscathed. He tapped the man, who turned the handle, on the shoulder and the man stopped. He walked out toward the front of the gun, and as the smoke cleared, he noticed small plumes of other smoke coming from the ground only ten meters in front of the gun.

He looked back at the soldier. "Shoot it again — one turn."

The soldier did as he ordered, and Gonzalez saw the bullets fall to the ground only a few meters from the end of the barrel. He walked out and kneeled down to pick one up, but it was too hot to the touch. He stood back up and looked down the road at Sosa, who turned his horse the other direction and rode quickly to the other Gatling gun, which was still firing rapidly.

"Cease fire!" He yelled as he dismounted, and then stood there glaring out into the field at the many workers who stood like statues. Chavón ran out in front of the gun, and like Gonzalez, noticed the smoking bullets on the ground, just a few meters out. He looked up at Sosa, who already knew what was happening, and amidst his fiery rage, he whispered his name through clenched teeth. "Molina!"

Just as Sosa was back on his horse, he spurred it back to the entrance to the lane, and pulled his pistol from its holster. Before he could make his command, the many field workers knelt to the ground, pushed the soil away and uncovered a rifle wrapped in a blanket. They rose quickly to their feet, and before the armed soldiers could begin their charge, the workers opened fire, and Sosa's men dropped like rag dolls.

Sosa ordered all of his men, on foot and on horseback, to engage, and he and Chavón joined in the charge. His wall of *policía* rolled like a tidal wave into the fields, firing back when they could, but most of them were cut down by bullets. Eventually Enrique joined in the fight, sending arrows into the chests of men who dared come in his direction.

Dutton spurred his horse across the field and when he got to the courtyard, he gave the guard the official nod, and the man turned the crank handle sending a storm of bullets down the lane, causing horses to rear and men to fall. Sosa and Chavón spurred their horses out of the lane and into the field, and Enrique was quick to fire an arrow, hitting a running Chavón in the thigh.

He screamed in agony, and turned back with a glare to seek out his enemy. But as he stood there on his mount, his courage was short-lived as Enrique was quick to nock another arrow, and as quick as he released, he watched the elite fighter suck in a breath as the arrow penetrated his chest.

Sosa turned to witness this defeat and he fired his pistol at Enrique. The *Criollo* fell to the ground after a bullet whizzed by his ear, and quickly sought cover on the other side of the palm tree. He nocked another arrow but the bullets kept splintering beside the tree and he couldn't get clear to make the shot. Eventually the bullets stopped, and when he peeked around he saw Sosa toss his empty pistol to the ground and spur his horse back toward the road. When there he quickly dismounted and took a pistol off of a dead soldier, stuck it under his belt, then grabbed another.

Rather than go off after him, Enrique looked around to see what else was happening, and was relieved to see that Dutton had retreated back and was no longer on horseback, but on one knee firing his rifle. Many of Sosa's men lay dead or wounded, and the ones that did make it through found themselves in a hand-to-hand fight, with either one of the workers, or Pang.

Pang was much quicker at subduing them, but Enrique was impressed to see that the people learned very well how to defend themselves, and caught many of the soldiers by surprise with punches and kicks that disabled them quickly.

Enrique was also pleased to see that the Gatling gun operators were not that busy, only shooting when the opportunity came, and did a very good job of keeping the lane clear.

It wasn't long before all of Sosa's men started to retreat, and whenever he witnessed this, he yelled out in a rage. "What are you doing! Get back in the fight!"

But the men would have none of it, including Gonzalez. If they found a horse, they mounted and ran. If one of the soldiers was lucky enough, he doubled up with another rider. It wasn't long before Sosa's attention was not on the *hacienda,* but shooting his own deserters. He succeeded several times, and when he found Gonzalez, he shot him three times in the back, only stopping long enough to watch the newly promoted lieutenant fall from his horse and to his death.

Dutton quickly intervened and fired a shot toward Sosa, knocking him down. After that all of the shooting stopped as everyone watched with anticipation to see if Sosa would get back up, or if the threat to Sonora was finally over.

"Keep trying!" Amado yelled. "You will get it!"

Felipe had found a spool of wire in the wine cellar, and he was sure that he could use a piece of it to pick the lock. Amado and Javier loved his idea, but the other children, having heard the gunshots, would have no part in it and tried to encourage them not to go. But the boys were trained soldiers — trained to fight, and the adrenaline within them could not be contained.

Felipe kept fishing with the wire inside the keyhole, his eyes wide and his concentration intense.

"Come on Felipe!" Amado yelled.

Eventually they all heard a click and Felipe stopped and looked at Amado with surprise. Amado grabbed the lock and pulled down and it opened. The three boys jumped triumphantly and ran up the stairs into the hallway of the *casa.* After they ran down the full length of the hall, they could not get past the study without being seen. They stopped and looked at them in fear.

Emanuela was the first to see them and she jumped and ran toward the door. "Amado! Felipe! What are you doing?"

"We are fighters, not cowards!"

Constanza came forward, her face drawn with anger. "You are boys, not men. I will not watch you walk to your death and break our hearts."

Amado stood firm. "You cannot stop us."

As Amado ran out of the house, the other boys followed, and Emanuela ran after them.

"Emanuela!" Constanza yelled, trying to stop her, but Guadalupe was quick to grab Constanza's arm before she could get out of the doorway. They all watched in fear as Emanuela chased the boys across the courtyard to the workers' quarters, where the boys quickly grabbed their bows and arrows. As they ran toward the stable to take cover, Emanuela grabbed Javier and they fell to the ground. "No, Javier," she cried. "I will not let you do this."

The boy kicked and screamed. "Let me go!"

She took the bow and arrow from him but she could not hold him any longer, and he ran to the corner of the stable, where the other two boys hid and peeked around into the fray. She dropped the bow and arrow and ran to them, if for nothing else, to seek shelter for herself. After she stopped and knelt down, she looked over the boys' heads to see that all of the shooting had stopped and that Sosa's men were retreating. Then she saw what had all of their attention: Sosa was on the ground.

"Do you see him?" Felipe said. "Maybe he is already dead?"

"No," Amado responded. "I am going to kill him."

Dutton got back on his horse and rode quickly to the guards at the Gatling gun, all the while keeping an eye on Sosa. He dismounted then slapped his horse on the rump, causing it to trot off. After getting a good look at where Sosa lay, he knelt down behind the right wheel and aimed his rifle in that direction.

"You boys did good," Dutton said.

"Gracias, señor," one of the guards said. "Do you think he is dead?"

"We will find out very shortly."

Enrique looked back at Dutton and Dutton nodded, and the *Criollo* got on his feet, with an arrow nocked, and started walking toward Sosa. He took five short, slow steps toward him before he saw his legs move. Enrique stopped and stood straight and as Sosa rose to his elbows, Enrique pulled back on the bowstring.

Dutton was quick to aim his rifle, but he

refrained until he knew more of what Enrique was going to do. Just as he was sure Enrique would send an arrow into the man's white tunic, a woman's voice cried out.

"Amado!" Everyone turned to see Amado running out into the lane and Emanuela chasing after him.

"Amado!" Enrique yelled. "Emanuela! No go back!"

Amado would not listen, and when he stopped to nock an arrow they all looked to see Sosa on his feet, limping, a bloody wound on his thigh and one on his left bicep. He walked slowly, mouth agape, with a gun hanging low in his right hand. He looked ahead at Amado and grinned then laughed, and quickly raised the gun and shot aimlessly. He no more than shot when Amado's arrow hit him in the thigh and he fell to his knee screaming in agony. Enrique also shot an arrow that hit Sosa in the center of his chest, which caused him to buckle forward, grasping the arrow with one hand, but he still stood there on one knee, glaring. All were amazed to see him rise slowly back to his feet, but he had dropped the gun, and started stumbling forward.

Dutton took careful aim with the rifle and fired off one round that hit Sosa in the stomach and sent him flying backward. Everyone was sure now that Sosa was done in. He had two arrows stuck in him, one in a vital place, and certainly the loss of a lot of blood from his other wounds.

The air grew quiet around them as they all kept an eye on the dying tyrant. Dutton stood beside the wheel of the Gatling gun, as did the guards, who stepped out to their left to see the miracle they all had hoped to see. But suddenly Sosa moved again, and all stood still as he rolled to his side, raised his head, and glared back at them with his eyes half closed. Slowly and amazingly he rose to his knees, grimacing at the pain from his wounds, arrows sticking out of his chest and thigh, and the bloody wounds that soaked his white uniform, he looked more like a corpse awakened from the dead.

Dutton raised his rifle back to his shoulder, ready to finish him off, but as Sosa got to his feet, and started to walk and laugh, he thought better to let the man bleed and suffer.

Amongst his laughing was coughing, and he spat blood, then glared around at all of them. Though he spoke with a slur, his words were still very clear. "You really think you can kill me?" He laughed and bared his bloody teeth, but then he looked straight ahead and his face grew long as though he saw a ghost. Before anyone could acknowledge what he saw, there were blasts from the Gatling gun as it rolled and riddled Sosa with bullets. He stood there amidst the firestorm, his body bobbing around like a scarecrow in the wind as bullets penetrated every limb, head and torso, and not until it stopped, did he finally fall facedown to the ground.

After the smoke from the gun had cleared everyone looked back to see Guadalupe Rojas releasing the crank handle of the Gatling gun. With a look as fierce as any general, she walked out from behind the gun and into the lane, and marched straight toward Sosa's bloody body. When she got there she stood above him, and with her foot she turned him over to his back. His eyes were still open, but blood poured from his mouth and nostrils, and from the many bullet wounds. She leaned forward and spat on him.

Before she could reap any more glory a cry came out from near the stable. Everyone looked to find Amado lying over Emanuela. *"Mi hermana! Mi hermana!"*

Enrique was quick to drop his bow and run to her side. He knelt down quickly and put a hand under her head. Her eyes were closed, and he could see a bloody spot at the top of her abdomen. A crowd quickly gathered around them as he felt her neck for a pulse, then looked up with wide eyes. "She is still alive!" Enrique said. "Quickly, help me get her into the house and get a doctor!"

Enrique cradled her as Dutton put a hand over the wound to add pressure. As he carried her, Enrique leaned forward and whispered to her. "I've got you now. Ema, it is me, Enrique. I got you."

Her eyes flickered and opened slightly. "Enrique?"

The *Criollo* smiled and tears welled in his eyes. "*Si,* Ema, it is me."

In all her weakness she found a slight smile. "You — you called me Ema."

"*Si . . . si, mi amor.* I love you."

Chapter Fifteen

Enrique sat at Emanuela's bedside, holding her hand while she slept. He had been there ever since the doctor had left, with a prognosis that she would be very weak from the loss of blood, and that she needed rest, but there still were many risks, and all they could do was let her sleep and pray.

Constanza paid them a visit, along with Dutton and Pang, and her report was good, that the wounded were few, and that there were no fatalities.

"It is unbelievable," Dutton said, "that so many bullets could fly, but so few got hurt."

Constanza assured them that it was all because of the training, and the hope and confidence brought on by their presence. Whether they were three or four, it did not matter, it was the legend — the legend of *El Trio* that gave them this hope and confidence.

"Now wait a minute," Dutton said. "It

wasn't just us, those Gatling guns misfired. I guess it helped that we took the good ammunition, but whatever they got a hold of sure didn't work." Dutton pulled a cartridge out of his vest pocket, and unsheathed his knife. With the knife, he pried the lead bullet out of the casing, then poured the contents of the casing out onto the table.

They all looked on with curiosity.

"I retrieved one of these bullets to see what was wrong," Dutton said, "and look there . . . filled mostly with cloth, and maybe only five grains of black powder."

"Is that not good?" Pang said.

Dutton laughed. "Good for us maybe, but not for them. A .50 caliber bullet has 70 grains of powder, and what little is here was barely enough to get the bullet out of the barrel. Somebody sold them some bad ammunition. But what I can't figure, is how the hell the people in the fields knew about it?"

Constanza laughed. "When we were helping the wounded out of the fields, one of the men told me about an old man who came to the *hacienda,* right before midnight last night. He rode in on a burro, and went to the workers' quarters and told them that his name was Ortiz Molina, and that he was a gunsmith. He said that he was hired by

Sosa to repair the Gatling guns, and supply them with ammunition. He assured them not to worry, that the ammunition would not be good, and that they should not fear the guns. Just like *El Trio,* the people thought of him as a man sent from God."

Dutton shook his head and grinned. "Well I'll be damned."

When the sun was up the next morning, Enrique woke to a crowing rooster, and to the moaning and squirming of Emanuela. He sat up in his chair, and then quickly stood up and grabbed her hand.

"Ema? Are you all right?"

She moved her head from side to side then opened her eyes slowly and eventually she looked directly at Enrique.

"Ema," Enrique said. "It is me."

"Enrique . . . *que pasó*?"

"You were hurt, but you are okay now. You must lay still and rest."

"Amado . . . is he okay?"

"Si," Enrique smiled. "He is okay. Everyone is okay."

She blinked her sleepy eyes. "Sosa?"

Enrique took a deep breath then let it out slowly. "No one will ever have to worry about him again."

At that moment Constanza walked into

the room with the doctor.

Enrique turned to greet them. "She is awake."

"Good," the doctor said. "I will check her wound and change her bandage."

Constanza grabbed Enrique's hand. "Why don't you come down for breakfast? Señor Dutton and Pang are both there, and Sereno. I would like to talk to all of you."

Enrique looked back at Emanuela.

"Don't worry," Constanza said, grabbing Enrique's arm and pulling him toward the door. "She will be fine."

After a hearty spread of eggs, peppers, tomatoes, and tortillas, the four men sipped on coffee with Constanza and Jose as they talked about the future of the *hacienda*. There was now a light in her eyes that had not been there before. Though she had lost a lot, to have the strength now to carry on meant everything to those who made their living at *Hacienda de Ramírez.* She talked of the many new business relationships that have opened up since Sosa's demise — that everyone is free to make their own choices based on their own good judgment and will. She had long wanted to export oranges and cotton, but could not because of the enormous taxes that Sosa had imposed at the closest port in Bahía Kino. Sure, they could have tried to ship them farther to the south, outside of Sosa's influence, but someone always caught them before they could make it out of Sonora. There were none of those worries now, and she thanked all of the men for the prosperity that they brought to her home and to her people.

Dutton was just glad that she no longer called them *El Trio.* Though he supposed he shouldn't let it bother him, he nodded toward Sereno, and mentioned how integral a part he played in the killing of Valdar. Constanza was glad to hear to whole story, but she also convinced them that the legend was too important to disrupt, to let it go, that it could all be their little secret.

She wondered, too, what all of their plans were now, and of course, she finally remembered that in the first place Enrique's visit was to locate his grandfather. She insisted that since the town was now celebrating the collapse of Sosa's regime, that people would not be so afraid to talk, and that his grandfather was surely somewhere in the city.

Enrique nodded. "I hope you are right. Before I leave, I will try to go and find him."

"Will Sereno be going with you?"

Sereno smiled and looked at Enrique.

"Yes," Enrique said. "When he was a boy

I used to call him my little Papago shadow. Wherever I went, he went with me. Other than the fact that we've all grown up, not much has changed. He is my brother, and I like to know he is close."

Constanza nodded then looked at the Chinaman. "And what about you, Señor Pang. What will you do?"

"I would like to go to sea and visit Mother China," Pang said, "but I am sure by the time I get back to Tucson I would get another telegram telling me that Enrique was in trouble, and I would have to come back here to help him."

Everyone laughed and Enrique tossed his cloth napkin at Pang.

"No," Pang said, "I believe I will stay and help Enrique look for his grandfather. Maybe he would appreciate the assistance."

Enrique grinned and nodded. "*Si,* I would, very much."

"I'll stay, too," Dutton said. "Somebody needs to hang around you boys who goes heals."

Pang shook his head. "I have never had a need for a gun, and never will."

Dutton winked at all of them. "Never know, there might be a day."

"What about your brother?" Enrique said. "Isn't he expecting you back in Missouri?"

Dutton grunted. "Well, he wants me back, I'm sure, but I doubt he expects anything. No, I'll write him a telegram. Maybe tell him I fell in love or something."

Pang laughed. "He would not believe that. No woman would ever find you that attractive."

"I didn't say *she* fell in love."

Everyone laughed out loud.

"Speaking of love," Constanza said, looking at Enrique. "What about Emanuela?"

Enrique paused and nodded. "We have much to talk about."

"Si," Constanza said. "It is always best to give things plenty of time." She glanced around the table at all of them. "But just so you know, you will always have a home here should you want to stay, or visit. And now, I must get to my business at hand. We have much work to do to rebuild our community."

Fernando and Guadalupe walked hand in hand down the lane under the palms, and then off into the orange grove, watching the workers tend to their duties, many of them smiling and sharing the joy of their newfound freedom.

"It is a nice place here," Guadalupe said. "Señora Ramírez is good to you. Maybe we should stay?"

"I am not sure I could," Fernando said. "Once the trust is gone, there is always that hint of doubt, and it is hard to live with."

"I know what you mean."

"I have heard that there are many great things happening in California. San Diego, Los Angeles. Señora Ramírez said that she would write a letter of recommendation should I want to leave."

Guadalupe stopped and turned to face Fernando. "That is very good. We could both go and make a new start."

Fernando smiled. "Yes, and we are much wiser now, and we will be very careful what we choose to do and who we associate with."

"How will you know?"

Fernando glanced around the *hacienda,* at the workers, and at the guards, all people who have stood loyal to Señora Ramírez. "I have known a lot of good people. People who can be trusted. I will always have those to compare."

Guadalupe nodded. "*Si,* I believe you are right." But suddenly a gloomy fear swept through her, and she looked away in thought.

"Mi amor," Fernando said. "What is it?"

She looked back into his eyes. "What about me, Fernando? Are you sure you can forgive all that I have done?"

Fernando rubbed his fingertips into her hair, then kissed her gently on the lips. They hugged each other tight, and in their embrace he said, "I have no idea what you are talking about."

Enrique kissed Emanuela on the forehead and looked into her eyes. "You rest. I am going into town to see if I can get any leads on my grandfather."

"Enrique," she said, grabbing on to his hand. "I don't want you to worry about me. Maybe it is better that you not stay."

Her statement confused him. "What are you talking about?"

She cleared her throat. "Do you not realize your destiny? You and your friends, you have a gift. A gift that is too valuable to too many people. Staying in one place is not for you."

Enrique rubbed at his mouth then put his hands on his hips. "But what about us?"

"It is because I love you that I am letting you go. I cannot keep you from what you're born to do. That would not be right."

The *Criollo* grabbed her hand and squeezed it tightly. He choked back any emotion that welled inside of him, then leaned forward and kissed her on the forehead. After he leaned back up, he looked deep into her glassy eyes. "I guess I will be going then."

"*Mucho cuidado,* Enrique."

Enrique nodded. "Good-bye, Ema." He let go of her hand, then turned and left the room.

When Enrique walked into the courtyard after leaving the *casa,* Dutton, Pang, and Sereno were all mounted on their horses waiting for him. But before he mounted his own horse, he heard a voice calling his name, and looked down toward the workers' quarters to see Amado running toward him. He decided to wait for the boy, and by the time he got there he was out of breath from running.

"Amado," Enrique said, "what is it?"

"Are you leaving?"

Enrique smiled. "Yes."

Amado's face grew long. "Felipe . . . he told me that you were looking for Isidro."

Enrique shared a serious glance with the three men, and then looked back at Amado. "*Si,* I was told you didn't know anything."

"Well . . . I am sorry, but I was not telling the truth. I was still afraid of Sosa, but now that he is gone, I am not afraid of anyone anymore."

Enrique smiled. *"Bien. Muy bien."*

"Sosa had sent him to *Casa del Norte,* but when he learned that you knew he was there, he had him . . . well, deported."

"Deported?"

"*Si,* but I don't know where."

"Do you have any idea who might know?"

"There is this man, in Mexico City, who helped hide people for Sosa."

"Mexico City? What was this man's name?"

"Señor Hector Contreras. I only saw him when I was working, at *Cantina de El Manadero.* He would come up here for work. That is all I know."

Enrique smiled and rubbed Amado's head. "*Gracias,* Amado."

"Does that help you?"

"Si," Enrique nodded. "That helps a lot."

Enrique mounted his horse and the four men waved good-bye to Amado. As they rode down the lane, Enrique glanced over at Dutton. "Mexico City?"

Dutton shrugged. "Hey, just be glad it's not Hong Kong."

"And just what is wrong with Hong Kong?" Pang said.

"It has a lot of Chinamen," Dutton said. "And besides that, lots of water between here and there."

"Maybe it would do you good to grow some sea legs."

"My legs are fine just where they are."

"All right, all right," Enrique said. "Let's forget about all of that right now."

Just as they were riding away, a man wearing a broad sombrero rode down the lane toward them. He was dressed similar to the field hands, with brown vest over white clothing, and a blanket draped over his shoulder. He stopped when he reached them.

"Are you the men of *El Trio*?" the man asked.

"Who is asking?" Dutton said.

"My name is Jorge Vázquez. Colonel Raul Vázquez was my brother."

"I am sorry about your brother," Enrique said.

Jorge reached behind him and grabbed a saddle bag, then tossed it to Enrique. The *Criollo* caught it and looked at it with surprise. "What is this?"

"My brother gave it to me to hide. He told me to never look inside, and that if anything ever happened to him, to bring it to you. My duty is done."

Before they could say anything Jorge turned and rode away. Enrique shared a look of curiosity with his friends, and then unbuckled the latches on the saddlebag. He looked inside first, then reached in and pulled out a leather bag, tied at the top, and it jingled. He tossed the bag to Dutton, who caught it, then reached inside and pulled out two more.

Dutton untied the cord at the top of the bag, opened it, and poured gold coins out into his hand. He looked back at the others with rounded eyes.

"Where did this come from?" Enrique said.

"I think I know," Dutton said, putting the coins back into the bag. "It was the money Sosa used to buy the Gatling guns. Colonel Vázquez had confiscated it, and he died for it."

Pang shook his head. "Sounds like unlucky money to me."

Enrique nodded. "I agree. What do we do with it?"

Dutton tossed the sack back to Enrique. "Doesn't matter to me. You know I have never been in this for the money. You hang on to it, I'm sure you'll find a good place for it."

As Enrique was putting the sacks of coins back into the saddle bag, Fernando and Guadalupe walked up to them.

"Hola, amigos," Fernando said. "Are you all leaving?"

"Si," Enrique said. "What about you?"

"We are leaving, too. Going to California. Going to start over. You know, make up for all of the years that Sosa took from us."

Guadalupe hugged Fernando's arm and smiled at all of the men. "But first, we are going to renew our vows."

Dutton nodded and grinned. "I'd say that's the best place to start."

Dutton looked back at Enrique, who raised his eyebrows. They each looked at Pang and Sereno, who also nodded their agreement. Enrique turned back to Fernando and Guadalupe and tossed them the saddle bag. Fernando caught it.

"What is this?" Fernando said.

"It's a wedding present," Enrique said.

Fernando and Guadalupe looked at the bag with surprise, and then looked solemnly back at the men. *"Gracias."*

Dutton tipped his hat, and then the four men all looked at each other.

"I think this calls for a beer at the *cantina.*" Enrique said.

"Now that's the best idea I've heard since I got to Mexico!" Dutton said, and then spurred his horse. The others were quick to join him, and before long they were loping down the road and through the streets of Hermosillo, enjoying what was left of the day and forgetting about what to do and where to go next. For now, they decided, it was just good to live in the moment.

ABOUT THE AUTHOR

Steven Law comes from a family of storytellers that inspired him with both folklore and the written word, all which derived from sources from their pioneer days to the novels of Mark Twain and Laura Ingalls Wilder. During college Steven felt inspired to write his first novel, which a constant busy schedule forced him to put on hold. After receiving a bachelor's degree in business administration, Steven spent several years in corporate America, and he also nearly completed a master's degree in business education. Increasingly disenchanted with his career and course work, he dropped out of graduate school to devote his life to writing. While struggling to make a name for himself, Steven worked as a community newspaper reporter, a columnist, and a freelance Web publicist for writers and writing organizations. For more than fourteen years he has worked with several acclaimed authors, such as Pulitzer Prize finalist S. C. Gwynne, *New York Times* bestseller Stephen Harrigan, *New York Times* columnist Peter Applebome, and the late Elmer Kelton.

Now a successful novelist, Steven lives in the Missouri Ozarks with his son, Tegan, two cats named Pepper and Sylvester, and a shih tzu named Obi. *Brave Sonora* is his sixth novel.

Visit his website at www.stevenlaw.com.

The employees of Thorndike Press hope you have enjoyed this Large Print book. All our Thorndike, Wheeler, and Kennebec Large Print titles are designed for easy reading, and all our books are made to last. Other Thorndike Press Large Print books are available at your library, through selected bookstores, or directly from us.

For information about titles, please call:
(800) 223-1244

or visit our Web site at:
http://gale.cengage.com/thorndike

To share your comments, please write:

Publisher
Thorndike Press
10 Water St., Suite 310
Waterville, ME 04901